Southern Christmas

Southern Christmas

Literary Classics
of the
Holidays

edited by
Judy Long
&
Thomas Payton

d

HILL STREET PRESS   ATHENS, GEORGIA

HILL STREET PRESS
Published by Hill Street Press, LLC
191 East Broad Street
Suite 209
Athens, Georgia 30601-2848
www.hillstreetpress.com

3 5 7 9 10 8 6 4 2

ISBN # 1-892514-08-7

Copyright © 1998 by Hill Street Press, LLC

LIBRARY OF CONGRESS CATALOG # 98-074031

Printed in the United States of America by R.R. Donnelley & Sons, Inc.

The paper in this book contains a significant amount of
post-consumer recycled fiber.

Text and cover design by Anne Richmond Boston.

Contents

Christmas Day, 1863

MARY BOYKIN CHESNUT
(1823-1866)

Mary Boykin Chesnut was born Mary Boykin Miller in Statesburg, South Carolina on her grandparents' estate. At the age of seventeen she married James Chesnut, Jr. and spent most of the next seven years in Camden and at Mulberry, her husband's family plantation. Mary Chesnut accompanied her husband to Washington, D. C. in 1858 when he was elected to the U. S. Senate. James Chesnut resigned from the upper chamber to lead the secessionist movement in South Carolina, and the couple moved to Montgomery and Richmond where he served under Jefferson Davis. They eventually settled in Columbia, S.C. Mary Chesnut began keeping diary entries on February 15, 1861 and ended her account on August 2, 1865. She returned to her original work in 1881 and expanded and revised her diary which was published nineteen years after her death. In this entry from Chesnut's *A Diary from Dixie* (1905) she wrote of Christmas Day 1863.

*Y*esterday dined with the Prestons. Wore one of my handsomest Paris dresses (from Paris before the war). Three magnificent Kentucky generals were present, with Senator Orr from South Carolina, and Mr. Miles. General Buckner repeated a speech of Hood's to him to show how friendly they were. "I prefer a ride with you in the company of any woman in the world," Buckner had answered. "I prefer your company to that of any man, certainly," was Hood's reply. This became the standing joke of the dinner; it flashed up in every form. Poor Sam got out of it so badly, if he got out of it at all. General Buckner said patronizingly, "Lame excuses, all. Hood never gets out of any scrape—that is, unless he can fight out." Others dropped in after dinner; some without arms, some without legs; von Borcke, who can not speak because of a wound in his throat. Isabella said: "We have all kinds now, but a blind one." Poor fellows, they laugh at wounds. "And they yet can show many a scar."

We had for dinner oyster soup, besides roast mutton, ham, boned turkey, wild duck, partridge, plum pudding, sauterne, burgundy, sherry, and Madeira. There is life in the old land yet!

Letter To His Daughter

ROBERT E. LEE
(1797–1870)

Robert Edward Lee was born in Stratford County, Virginia, the son of
Revolutionary War hero, "Light Horse Harry" Lee and Anne Hill
Carter. He graduated from West Point in 1829, served in the engi-
neer corps and the Mexican War, and in 1852 was appointed
superintendent of West Point. He commanded the troops which
suppressed the John Brown Raid in 1859. In 1861 he resigned as
Colonel in the United States army, was appointed Commander-
in-Chief of the Virginia forces, and later of the Confederate army.
After the Civil War, Lee refused lucrative business offers, and
accepted the post of President of Washington University, now
Washington and Lee University. As a proponent of moderation,
and by his refusal to prolong conflict, Lee helped to restore the
Union. The following letter was published in *Recollections and
Letters of General Robert E. Lee* (1905) by his son Robert E. Lee,
Jr. In this 1866 letter, Lee bestowed a Christmas blessing on his
youngest child, Mildred Childe Lee, known within her family as
"Precious Life."

Lexington, Virginia, December 21, 1866.

*M*Y PRECIOUS LIFE: I was very glad to receive your
letter of the 15th inst., and to learn that you were well
and happy. May you be always as much so as is consis-
tent with your welfare here and hereafter, is my daily prayer. I was
much pleased, too that, while enjoying the kindness of your friends,
we were not forgotten. Experience will teach you that, notwith-
standing all appearances to the contrary, you will never receive
such a love as is felt for you by your father and mother. That lives

through your absence, difficulties, and time. Your own feelings will teach you how it should be returned and appreciated. I want to see you very much, and miss you at every turn, yet am glad of this opportunity for you to be with those, who, I know, will do all in their power to give you pleasure. I hope you will also find time to read and improve your mind. Read history, works of truth, not novels and romances. Get correct views of life, and learn to see the world in its true light. It will enable you to live pleasantly, to do good, and, when summoned sway, to leave without regret. Your friends here inquire constantly after you, and wish for your return. Mrs. White and Mrs. McElwee particularly regret your absence, and the former sends special thanks for your letter of remembrance. We get on in our usual way. Agnes takes good care of us, and is very thoughtful and attentive. She has not great velocity, but its systematic and quiet. After to-day, the mornings will begin to lengthen a little, and her trials to lessen. It is very cold, the ground is covered with six inches of snow, and the mountains, as far as the eye can reach in every direction, elevate their white crests as monuments of winter. This is the night for the supper for the repairs to the Episcopal church. Your mother and sisters are busy with their contributions. It is to take place at the hotel, and your brother, cousins, and father are to attend. On Monday-night (24th), the supper for the Presbyterian church is to be held at their lecture-room. They are to have music and every attraction. I hope both may be productive of good. But you know the Episcopalians are few in numbers and light in purse, and must be resigned to small returns. . . . I must leave your sisters a description of these feasts and also an account to the operation of the Reading Club. As far as I can judge, it is a great institution for the discussion of apples and chestnuts, but is quite innocent for the pleasures of literature. It, however, brings the young people together, and promotes sociability and conversation. Our feline companions are flourishing. Young Baxter is growing in gracefulness and favour, and gives cat-like evidence of future worth. He possesses the fashionable colour of "moonlight on the water," apparently a dingy hue of the kitchen, and is strictly aristocratic in appearance and conduct. Tom, surnamed, "The Nipper," from the manner in which he slaughters our enemies, the rats and mice, is admired for his gravity and sobriety, a s well as for his strict attention to the pursuits of his race. They both feel your absence sorely. Traveller and Custis are both well, and pursue their usual dignified gait and habits, and are not led away by the frivolous entertainments of lectures and concerts. All send united love, and all wish for your return. Remember me most kindly to Cousins Eleanor and George, John, Mary, Ida, and all at "Myrtle Grove," and to other kind friends when you meet them. Mrs. Grady carried yesterday to Mr. Charles Kerr, in Baltimore, a small package for you. Be careful of your health, and do not eat more than half the plum-puddings Cousin Eleanor has prepared for Xmas. I am glad to hear that your are fattening, and I hope you will reach 125 lbs. Think always of your father, who loves you dearly.

R.E. Lee.

P. S. 22d. — Rob arrived last night with "Lucy Long." He thinks it too bad you are way. He has not seen you for two years.

R.E. Lee.

Susie's Letter from Santa

MARK TWAIN (SAMUEL LANGHORNE CLEMENS (1835–1910)

Mark Twain was born Samuel Langhorne Clemens in Florida, Missouri, and at the age of four he moved to Hannibal, Missouri on the Mississippi River. Growing up, Twain absorbed everyday life in the river town, which provided the richest source of his literary material. When he was fourteen, Twain was apprenticed to two Hannibal printers and began writing sketches for his brother Orion's newspaper, *The Hannibal Journal*. Twain worked as a journeyman printer from 1853-1857 in various cities, including New York and Philadelphia. Drawn back to the Mississippi River, he then became a pilot's apprentice under Horace Bixby and worked as a steamboat pilot until the Civil War brought an end to river travel in 1861. Twain served briefly in the Confederate army, and then accompanied his brother Orion to the newly created Nevada Territory. When his attempts at silver mining failed, he became a reporter for *The Territorial Enterprise* in Virginia City, Nevada, and, in 1863, he first used the pseudonym "Mark Twain," a Mississippi River phrase meaning two fathoms deep. After moving to San Francisco, Twain continued to write, and his story "Jim Smiley and His Jumping Frog" (1865) was published in *The New York Saturday Press*. Twain became a national sensation and published his first book *The Celebrated Jumping Frog of Calaveras County* (1867), a collection of sketches. Twain settled with his family in Hartford, Connecticut in 1872 and traveled extensively in Europe. He launched a career as a lecturer and published numerous books that brought him great financial reward. These works included *Roughing It* (1872), *The Adventures of Tom Sawyer* (1876), *Life on the Mississippi* (1883), and *The Adventures of Huckleberry Finn* (1885). Despite the success of his books, Twain declared bankruptcy in 1894, and the following years were his most unfortunate. In 1896, his eldest daughter Susie died, followed by his wife Livy in 1904 and his youngest daughter Jean in 1909. Twain penned this Christmas letter from Santa Claus to his daughter Susie, born in 1872, during happier times.

Palace of St. Nicholas
In the Moon
Christmas Morning

$\mathcal{M}$y Dear Susie Clemens:

I have received and read all the letters which you and your little sister have written me by the hand of your mother and your nurses; I have also read those which you have little people have written me with your own hands—for although you did not use any characters that are in grown people's alphabet, you used the characters that all children in all lands on earth and in the twinkling stars use; and as all my subjects in the moon are children and use no characters but that, you will easily understand that I can read your and your baby sister's jagged and fantastic marks without trouble at all. But I had trouble with those letters which you dictated through your mother and the nurses, for I am a foreigner and cannot read English writing well. You will find that I made no mistakes about the things which you and the baby ordered in your *own* letters—I went down your chimney at midnight when you were asleep and delivered them all myself—and kissed both of you, too, because you are good children, well-trained, nice-mannered, and about the most obedient little people I ever saw. But in the letters which you dictated there are some words that I could not make out for certain, and one or two small orders which I could not fill because we ran out of stock. Our last lot of Kitchen-furniture for dolls has just gone to a poor little child in the North Star away up in the cold country about the Big Dipper. Your mama can show you that star and you will say: "Little Snow Flake" (for that is the child's name) "I'm glad that you got that furniture, for you need it more than I." That is, you must *write* that, with your own hand, and Snow Flake will write you an answer. If you only spoke it she wouldn't hear you. Make your letter light and thin, for the distance is great and the postage heavy.

There was a word or two in your mama's letter which I couldn't be certain of. I took it to be a "trunk full of doll's clothes." Is that it? I will call at your kitchen door just about nine o'clock this morning to inquire. But I must not see anybody and I must not speak to anybody but you. When the kitchen door bell rings George must be blindfolded and sent to open the door. Then he must go back to the dining-room or the china closet and take the cook with him. You must tell George that he must walk on tiptoe and not speak—otherwise he will die some day. Then you must go up to the nursery and stand on a chair or the nurse's bed and put your ear to the speaking tube that leads down to the kitchen and when I whistle through it you must speak in the tube and say, "Welcome, Santa Claus!" Then I will ask whether it was a trunk you ordered or not. If you say it was, I shall ask you what *color* you want the trunk to be. Your mama will help you to name a nice color and then you must tell me every single thing in detail which you may want the trunk to contain. Then when I say "Good bye and a Merry Christmas to my little Susie Clemens," you must say "Good bye, good old Santa Claus, I thank you very much and please tell Snow Flake I will look at her star tonight and she must look down here—I will be right in the West bay-window; and every fine night I will look at her star and say, 'I know somebody up there and *like* her too.'" Then you must go down into the library and make George close all the doors that open into the mainhall, and everybody must keep still for awhile. I will go to the moon and get those things and in a few minutes I will come down the chimney that belongs to the fireplace that is in the hall— if it is a trunk you want—because I couldn't get such a thing as a trunk down the nursery chimney, you know.

People may talk if they want, until they hear my footsteps in the hall. Then you tell them to keep quiet a little while till I go backup the chimney. Maybe you will not hear my footsteps at all—so you may go now and then and peep through the dining-room doors, and by and by you will see that thing which you want, right under that piano in the drawing-room—for I shall put it there. If I should leave any snow in the hall, you must tell George to sweep it into the fire-place, for I haven't time to do such things. George must not use a broom, but a rag—else he will die some day. You must watch George and not let him run into danger. If my boot should leave a stain on the marble, George must not holystone it away. Leave it there always in memory of my visit; and whenever you look at it or show it to anybody you must let it remind you to be a good little girl. Whenever you are naughty and somebody points to that mark which your good Santa Claus's boot made on the marble, what will you say, little Sweetheart?

Goodbye for a few minutes, till I come down to the world and ring the kitchen door-bell.

Your loving
Santa Claus
Whom people sometimes call The Man in the Moon.

Little Miss Sophie

ALICE DUNBAR-NELSON
(1875–1935)

Alice Dunbar-Nelson was born Alice Ruth Moore in New Orleans, Louisiana, where she spent the first twenty years of her life. Only one generation removed from slavery, Dunbar-Nelson was educated at Straight College, completing a two-year teacher-training program in 1891. Her first book, *Violets and Other Tales* (1895), a collection of short stories, sketches, essays, reviews, and poetry, was published when she was barely twenty years old. One of the most important aspects of Dunbar-Nelson's life was her teaching career, which she began in 1892 and continued with few interruptions until 1931. Dunbar-Nelson devoted an equal amount of time to her writing, working as a journalist, essayist, short story writer, and diarist. In 1895, poet Paul Laurence Dunbar fell in love with Dunbar-Nelson after seeing her photograph in an issue of *Boston Monthly Review*. He initiated an epistolary courtship with her, but they did not meet until 1897 when she moved to New York City to teach at a public school in Brooklyn. They married secretly in 1898, divorcing in 1902. In her honest portrayal of blacks and Creoles, Dunbar helped to educate a reading public conditioned to expect contrived dialect and racial stereotypes. Her second book, *The Goodness of St. Rocque and Other Stories* (1899), was the first collection of short stories published by a black woman in America. In that volume, Dunbar-Nelson included "Little Miss Sophie," the story of a last, unselfish Christmas gift.

⊥

When Miss Sophie knew consciousness again, the long, faint, swelling notes of the organ were dying away in distant echoes through the great arches of the silent church, and she was alone, crouching in a little, forsaken black heap at the altar of the Virgin. The twinkling tapers shone pityingly upon her, the beneficent smile of the white-robed Madonna seemed to whisper comfort. A long gust of chill air swept up the aisles, and Miss Sophie shivered not from cold, but from nervousness.

But darkness was falling, and soon the lights would be lowered, and the great massive door would be closed; so, gathering her thin little cape about her frail shoulders, Miss Sophie hurried out, and along the brilliant noisy streets home.

It was a wretched, lonely little room, where the cracks let the boisterous wind whistle through, and the smoky, grimy walls looked cheerless and unhomelike. A miserable little room in a miserable little cottage in one of the squalid streets of the Third District that nature and the city fathers seemed to have forgotten.

As bare and comfortless as the room was Miss Sophie's life. She rented these four walls from an unkempt little Creole woman, whose progeny seemed like the promised offspring of Abraham. She scarcely kept the flickering life in her pale little body by the unceasing toil of a pair of bony hands, stitching, stitching, ceaselessly, wearingly, on the bands and pockets of trousers. It was her bread, this monotonous, unending work; and though whole days and nights constant labour brought but the most meagre recompense, it was her only hope of life.

She sat before the little charcoal brazier and warmed her transparent, needle-pricked fingers, thinking meanwhile of the strange events of the day. She had been up town to carry the great, black bundle of coarse pants and vests to the factory and to receive her small pittance, and on the way home stopped in at the Jesuit Church to say her little prayer at the altar of the calm white Virgin. There had been a wondrous burst of music from the great organ as she knelt there, and overpowering perfume of many flowers, the glittering dazzle of many lights, and the dainty frou-frou made by the silken skirts of wedding guests. So Miss Sophie stayed to the wedding; for what feminine heart, be it ever so old and seared, does not delight in one? And why should not a poor little Creole old maid be interested too?

Then the wedding party had filed in solemnly, to the rolling, swelling tones of the organ. Important-looking groomsmen; dainty, fluffy, white-robed maids; stately, satin-robed, illusion-veiled bride, and happy groom. She leaned forward to catch a better glimpse of their faces. "Ah!" —

Those near the Virgin's altar who heard a faint sigh and rustle on the steps glanced curiously as they saw a slight black-robed figure clutched the railing and lean her head against it. Miss Sophie had fainted.

"I must have been hungry," she mused over the charcoal fire in her little room, "I must have been hungry;" and she smiled a wan smile, and busied herself getting her evening meal of coffee and bread and ham.

If one were given to pity, the first thought that would rush to one's lips at the sight of Miss Sophie would have been, "Poor little woman!" She had come among the bareness and sordidness of this neighbourhood five years ago, robed in crape, and crying with great sobs that seemed to shake the vitality out of her. Perfectly silent, too, she was about her former life; but for all that, Michel, the quartee grocer at the corner, and Madame Laurent, who kept the rabbe shop opposite, had fixed it all up between them, of her sad history and past glories. Not that they knew; but then Michel must invent something when the neighbours came to him as their fountain-head of wisdom.

One morning little Miss Sophie opened wide her dingy windows to catch the early freshness of the autumn wind as it whistled through the yellow-leafed trees. It was one of those calm, blue-misted, balmy, November days that New Orleans can have when all the rest of the country is fur-wrapped. Miss Sophie pulled her machine to the window, where the sweet, damp wind could whisk among her black locks.

Whirr, whirr, went the machine, ticking fast and lightly over the belts of the rough jeans pant. Whirr, whirr, yes, and Miss Sophie was actually humming a tune! She felt strangely light to-day.

"Ma foi," muttered Michel, strolling across the street to where

Madame Laurent sat sewing behind the counter on the blue and brown-checked aprons, "but the little ma'amselle sings. Perhaps she recollects."

"Perhaps," muttered the rabbe woman.

But little Miss Sophie felt restless. A strange impulse seemed drawing her up town, and the machine seemed to run slow, slow, before it would stitch all the endless number of jeans belts. Her fingers trembled with nervous haste as she pinned up the unwieldy black bundle of finished work, and her feet fairly tripped over each other in their eagerness to get to Claiborne Street, where she could board the up-town car. There was a feverish desire to go somewhere, a sense of elation, a foolish happiness that brought a faint echo of colour into her pinched cheeks. She wondered why.

No one noticed her in the car. Passengers on the Claiborne line are too much accustomed to frail little black-robed women with big, black bundles; it is one of the city's most pitiful sights. She leaned her head out of the window to catch a glimpse of the oleanders on Bayou Road, when her attention was caught by a conversation in the car.

"Yes, it's too bad for Neale, and lately married too," said the elder man. "I can't see what he is to do."

Neale! She pricked up her ears. That was the name of the groom in the Jesuit Church.

"How did it happen?" languidly inquired the younger. He was a stranger, evidently; a stranger with a high regard for the faultlessness of male attire.

"Well, the firm failed first; he didn't mind that much, he was so sure of his uncle's inheritance repairing his lost fortunes; but suddenly this difficulty of identification springs up, and he is literally on the verge of ruin."

"Won't some of you fellows who've known him all your lives do to identify him?"

"Gracious man, we've tried; but the absurd old will expressly stipulates that he shall be known only by a certain quaint Roman ring, and unless he has it, no identification, no fortune. He has given the ring away, and that settles it."

"Well, you're all chumps. Why doesn't he get the ring from the owner?"

"Easily said; but—it seems that Neale had some little Creole love-affair some years ago, and gave this ring to his dusky-eyed fiancée. You know how Neale is with his love-affairs, went off and forgot the girl in a month. It seems, however, she took it to heart,— so much so that he's ashamed to try to find her or the ring."

Miss Sophie heard no more as she gazed out into the dusty grass. There were tears in her eyes, hot blinding ones that wouldn't drop for pride, but stayed and scalded. She knew the story, with all its embellishment of heartaches. She knew the ring, too. She remembered the day she had kissed and wept and fondled it, until it seemed her heart must burst under its load of grief before she took it to the pawn-broker's that another might be eased before the end came,—that other her father. The little "Creole love affair" of Neale's had not always been poor and old and jaded-looking; but reverses must come, even Neale knew that, so the ring was at the Mont de Piété. Still he must have it, it was his; it would save him from disgrace and suffering and from bringing the white-gowned bride into sorrow. He must have it; but how?

There it was still at the pawn-broker's; no one would have such an odd jewel, and the ticket was home in the bureau drawer. Well, he must have it; she might starve in the attempt. Such a thing as going to him and telling him that he might redeem it was an impossibility. That good, straight-backed, stiff-necked Creole Blood would have risen in all its strength and choked her. No; as a present had the quaint Roman circlet been place upon her finger, as a present should it be returned.

The bumping car rode slowly, and the hot thoughts beat heavily in her poor little head. He must have the ring; but how— the ring—the Roman ring—the white-robed bride starving—she was going mad—ah yes—the church.

There it was, right in the busiest, most bustling part of the town, its fresco and bronze and iron quaintly suggestive of mediæval times. Within, all was cool and dim and restful, with the faintest whiff of lingering incense rising and pervading the gray arches. Yes, the Virgin would know and have pity; the sweet, white-robed Virgin at the pretty flower-decked altar, or the one away up in the niche, far above the golden dome where the Host was.

Titiche, the busybody of the house, noticed that Miss Sophie's bundle was larger than usual that afternoon. "Ah, poor woman!" sighed Titiche's mother, "she would be rich for Christmas."

The bundle grew larger each day, and Miss Sophie grew smaller. The damp, cold rain and mist closed the white-curtained window, but always there behind the sewing-machine drooped and bobbed the little black-robed figure. Whirr, whirr went the wheels, and the coarse jeans pants piled in great heaps at her side. The Claiborne Street car saw her oftener than before, and the sweet white Virgin in the flowered niche above the gold-domed altar smiled at the little supplicant almost every day.

"Ma foi," said the slatternly landlady to Madame Laurent and Michel one day, "I no see how she live! Eat? Nothin', nothin', almos', and las' night when it was so cold and foggy, eh? I hav' to mek him build fire. She mos' freeze."

Whereupon the rumour spread that Miss Sophie was starving herself to death to get some luckless relative out of jail for Christmas; a rumour which enveloped her scraggy little figure with a kind of halo to the neighbours when she appeared on the streets.

November had merged into December, and the little pile of coins was yet far from the sum needed. Dear God! How the money did have to go! The rent and the groceries and the coal, though to be sure, she used a precious bit of that. Would all the work and saving and skimping do good? Maybe, yes, maybe by Christmas.

Christmas Eve on Royal Street is no place for a weakling, for the shouts and carousals of the roisterers will strike fear into the bravest ones. Yet amid the cries and yells, the deafening blow of

horns and tin whistles, and the really dangerous fusillade of fire-
works, a little figure hurried along, one hand clutching tightly the
battered hat that the rude merry-makers had torn off, the other
grasping under the thin black cape a worn little pocketbook.

Into the Mont de Piété she ran breathless, eager. The ticket?
Here, worn, crumpled. The ring? It was not gone? No, thank
Heaven! It was a joy well worth her toil, she thought, to have it again.

Had Titiche not been shooting crackers on the banquette
instead of peering into the crack, as was his wont, his big, round
black eyes would have grown saucer-wide to see little Miss Sophie
kiss and fondle a ring, an ugly clumsy band of gold.

"Ah, dear ring," she murmured, "once you were his, and you
shall be his again. You shall be on his finger and perhaps touch his
heart. Dear ring, ma chère petite de ma cœur, chérie de ma cœur.
Je t'aime, je t'aime, oui, oui. You are his; you were mine once too.
To-night just one night, I'll keep you—then—tomorrow, you shall
go where you can save him."

The loud whistles and horns of the little ones rose on the balmy
air next morning. No one would doubt it was Christmas Day, even
if door and windows were open wide to let in cool air. Why, there
was Christmas even in the very look of the mules on the poky cars;
there was Christmas noise in the streets, and Christmas toys and
Christmas odours, savoury ones that made the nose wrinkle approv-
ingly, issuing from the kitchen. Michel and Madame Laurent
smiled greetings across the street at each other, and the salutation
from a passer-by recalled the many-progenied landlady to herself.

"Miss Sophie, well, po' soul, not ver' much Chris'mas for her.
Mais, I'll jus' call him in fo' to spen' the day with me. Eet'll cheer
her a bit."

It was so clean and orderly within the poor little room. Not a
speck of dust or a litter of any kind on the quaint little old-time high
bureau, unless you might except a sheet of paper lying loose with
something written on it. Titiche had evidently inherited his prying
propensities, for the landlady turned it over and read,—

Louis, — Here is the ring. I return it to you. I heard you needed it. I hope it comes not too late.

Sophie.

"The ring, where?" muttered the landlady. There it was, clasped between her fingers on her bosom, — a bosom white and cold, under a happy face. Christmas had indeed dawned for Miss Sophie.

Whistling Dick's Christmas Stocking

O. HENRY (WILLIAM SYDNEY PORTER)
(1862-1910)

O. Henry was born William Sydney Porter in Greensboro, North Carolina, where he spent the first twenty years of his life. In 1882 he moved to Texas, and for the next fifteen years worked at various jobs, including bookkeeper, drug clerk, and bank teller. It was there that he fulfilled a life-long dream to publish his skits and short sketches in his own humor paper, *The Rolling Stone*. The origins of his later themes, plots, and style are to be found in this weekly, but his efforts to keep it afloat led to his "borrowing" of funds from the bank where he was employed. O. Henry intended to replace the money, but he was tried for embezzlement and convicted in 1898. "Whistling Dick's Christmas Stocking" (1899), was written while he was in prison and mailed expectantly to *McClure's*, with the hope of earning money to buy his daughter, Margaret, a Christmas present. Porter used the money he received from the publication of this story, his first submitted using the pseudonym O. Henry, to buy Margaret the latest volumes of *Uncle Remus*. He liked the good old-fashioned and unsophisticated celebration of Christmas, and had no use for the story of which he said, "The only way you can tell it is a Christmas story is to look at the footnote which reads '["The incident in the above story happened on December 25th—Ed."]'" O. Henry was recognized as a master of short fiction, so his name was the inevitable choice for the award when, in 1919, Doubleday began publishing a selection of the year's best stories by American writers in American magazines. To have a story published in the *O. Henry Memorial Award Prize Stories* still symbolizes preeminence in the field of short story writing.

t was with much caution that Whistling Dick slid back the door of the box car, for Article 5716, City Ordinances, authorized (perhaps unconstitutionally) arrest on suspicion, and he was familiar of old with this ordinance. So, before climbing out, he surveyed the field with all the care of a good general.

He saw no change since his last visit to this big, alms-giving, long-suffering city of the South, the cold-weather paradise of the tramps. The levee where his freight car stood was pimpled with dark bulks of merchandise. The breeze reeked with the well-remembered, sickening smell of the old tarpaulins that covered bales and barrels. The dun river slipped along among the shipping with an oily gurgle. Far down toward Chalmette he could see the great bend in the stream outlined by the row of electric lights. Across the river Algiers lay, a long, irregular blot, made darker by the dawn which lightened the sky beyond. An industrious tug or two, coming for some early sailing-ship, gave a few appalling toots, that seemed to be the signal for breaking day. The Italian luggers were creeping nearer their landing, laden with early vegetables and shellfish. A vague roar, subterranean in quality, from dray wheels and street cars, began to make itself heard and felt; and the ferryboats, the Mary Anns of water craft, stirred sullenly to their menial morning tasks.

Whistling Dick's red head popped suddenly back into the car. A sight too imposing and magnificent for his gaze had been added to the scene. A vast, incomparable policeman rounded a pile of rice sacks and stood within twenty yards of the car. The daily miracle of the dawn, now being performed above Algiers, received the flattering attention of this specimen of municipal official splendor. He gazed with unbiased dignity at the faintly glowing colors until, at last, he turned to them his broad back, as if convinced that legal interference was not needed, and the sunrise might proceed unchecked. So he turned his face to the rice bags, and drawing a flat flask from an inside pocket, he placed it to his lips and regarded the firmament.

Whistling Dick, professional tramp, possessed a half friendly acquaintance with this officer. They both loved music. Still, he did not care, under the present circumstances, to renew the acquaintance. There is a difference between meeting a policeman upon a lonely street corner and whistling a few operatic airs with him, and being caught by him crawling out of a freight car. So Dick waited, as even a New Orleans policeman must move on some time—perhaps it is a retributive law of nature—and before long "Big Fritz" majestically disappeared between the trains of cars.

Whistling Dick waited as long as his judgment advised, and then slid swiftly to the ground. Assuming as far as possible the air of an honest laborer who seeks his daily toil, he moved across the network of railway lines, with the intention of making his way by quiet Girod Street to a certain bench in La Fayette Square, where, according to appointment, he hoped to rejoin a pal known as "Slick," this adventurous pilgrim having preceded him by one day, in a cattle car into which a loose slat had enticed him.

As Whistling Dick picked his way where night still lingered among the big, reeking musty warehouses, he gave way to the habit that had won for him his title. Subdued, yet clear, with each note as true and liquid as a bobolink's, his whistle tinkled about the dim, cold mountains of brick like drops of fain falling into a hidden pool. He followed an air, but it swam mistily into a swirling current of improvisation. You could cull out the trill of mountain brooks, the staccato of green rushes shivering above chilly lagoons, the pipe of sleepy birds.

Rounding a corner, the whistler collided with a mountain of blue and brass.

"So," observed the mountain calmly, "you are alreaty pack. Und dere vill not pe frost before two veeks yet. Und you haf forgotten how to vistle. Dere was a valse not in dot last bar."

"Watcher know about it?" said Whistling Dick, with tentative familiarity; "you wit yer little Cherman-ban nixcumrous chunes. Watcher know about music? Pick yer ears, and listen agin. Here's de way I whistled it—see?"

He puckered his lips, but the big policeman held up his hand.

Shtop," he said, "und learn der right way. Und learn also dot a rolling shtone gan't vistle for a cent."

Big Fritz's heavy mustache rounded into a circle, and from its depths came a sound deep and mellow as that from a flute. He repeated a few bars of the air the tramp had been whistling. The rendition was cold, but correct, and he emphasized the note he had taken exception to.

"Dot p is p natural, and not p vlat. Py der vay, you petter pe glad I meet you. Von hour later, and I vould haf to put you in a gage to vistle mit der chail pirds. Der orders are to bull all der pums afder sunrise."

"To which?"

"To bull der pums—eferybody mitout fisible means. Dirty days is der price, or fifteen tollars."

"Is dat straight, or a game you givin' me?"

"It's der pest tip you efer had. I gif it to you pecause I pelief you are not so bad as der rest. Und pecause you gan vistle 'Die Freischutz' bezzer dan I myself gan. Don't run against any more bolicemans aroundt der corners, but go avay vrom town a few tays. Goot-pye."

So Madame Orleans had at last grown weary of the strange and ruffled brood that came yearly to nestle beneath her charitable pinions.

After the big policeman had departed, Whistling Dick stood for an irresolute minute, feeling all the outraged indignation of a delinquent tenant who is ordered to vacate his premises. He had pictured to himself a day of dreamful ease when he should have joined his pal; a day of lounging on the wharf, munching the bananas and cocoanuts scattered in unloading the fruit steamers; and then a feast along the free-lunch counters from which the easy-going owners were too good-natured or too generous to drive him away, and afterward a pipe in one of the little flowery parks and a snooze in some shady corner of the wharf. But here was stern order to exile, and one that he knew must be obeyed. So, with a wary eye open for the gleam of brass buttons, he began his retreat toward a rural refuge. A few days in the country need not necessarily prove disastrous. Beyond the possibility of a slight nip of frost, there was no formidable evil to be looked for.

However, it was with a depressed spirit that Whistling Dick passed the old French market on his chosen route down the river. For safety's sake, he still presented to the world his portrayal of the part of the worthy artisan on his way to labor. A stallkeeper in the market, undeceived, hailed him by the generic name of his ilk, and "Jack" halted, taken by surprise. The vender, melted by this proof of his own acuteness, bestowed a foot of Frankfurter and half a loaf, and thus the problem of breakfast was solved.

When the streets, from topographical reasons, began to shun the river bank, the exile mounted to the top of the levee, and on its well-trodden path pursued his way. The suburban eye regarded him with cold suspicion. Individuals reflected the stern spirit of the city's heartless edict. He missed the seclusion of the crowded town and the safety he could always find in the multitude.

At Chalmette, six miles upon his desultory way, there suddenly menaced him a vast and bewildering industry. A new port was being established; the dock was being built, compresses were going up; picks and shovels and barrows struck at him like serpents from every side. An arrogant foreman bore down upon him, estimating his muscles with the eye of a recruiting sergeant. Brown men and black men all about him were toiling away. He fled in terror.

By noon he had reached the country of the plantations, the great, sad, silent levels bordering the mighty river. He overlooked fields of sugar-cane so vast that their farthest limits melted into the sky. The sugar-making season was well advanced, and the cutters were at work; the wagons creaked drearily after them; the negro teamsters inspired the mules to greater speed with mellow and sonorous imprecations. Dark green groves, blurred by the blue of distance, showed where the plantation houses stood. The tall chimneys of the sugar-mills caught the eye miles distant, like lighthouses at sea.

At a certain point Whistling Dick's unerring nose caught the scent of frying fish. Like a pointer to a quail, he made his way down the levee side straight to the camp of a credulous and ancient fisherman, whom he charmed with song and story, so that he dined like an admiral, and then like a philosopher annihilated the worst three hours of the day by a nap under the trees.

When he awoke and again continued his hegira, a frosty sparkle in the air had succeeded the drowsy warmth of the day, and as this portent of a chilly night translated itself to the brain of Sir Peregrine, he lengthened his stride and bethought him of shelter. He traveled a road that faithfully followed the convolutions of the levee, running along its base, but whither he knew not. Bushes and rank grass crowded it to the wheel ruts, and out of this ambuscade the pests of the lowlands swarmed after him, humming a keen, vicious soprano. And as the night grew nearer, although colder, the whine of the mosquitos became a greedy, petulant snarl that shut out all other sounds. To his right, against the heavens, he saw a green light moving, and, accompanying it, the masts and funnels of a big incoming steamer, moving as upon a screen at a magic-lantern show. And there were mysterious marshes at his left, out of which came queer gurgling cries and a choked croaking. The whistling vagrant struck up a merry warble to offset these melancholy influences, and it is likely that never before, since Pan himself jigged it on his reeds, had such sounds been heard in those depressing solitudes.

A distant clatter in the rear quickly developed into the swift beat of horses' hoofs, and Whistling Dick stepped aside into the dew-wet grass to clear the track. Turning his head, he saw approaching a fine team of stylish grays drawing a double surrey. A stout man with a white mustache occupied the front seat, giving all his attention to the rigid lines in his hands. Behind him sat a placid, middle-aged lady and a brilliant looking girl hardly arrived at young ladyhood. The laprobe had slipped partly from the knees of the gentleman driving, and Whistling Dick saw two stout canvas bags between his feet—bags such as, while loafing in cities, he had seen warily transferred between express wagons and bank doors. The remaining space in the vehicle was filled with parcels of various sizes and shapes.

As the surrey swept even with the sidetracked tramp, the bright-eyed girl, seized by some merry, madcap impulse, leaned out toward him with a sweet, dazzling smile, and cried, "Mer-ry Christmas!" in a shrill, plaintive treble.

Such a thing had not often happened to Whistling Dick, and he felt handicapped in devising the correct response. But lacking time for reflection, he let his instinct decide, and snatching off his battered derby, he rapidly extended it at arm's length, and drew it back with a continuous motion, and shouted a loud, but ceremonious, "Ah, there!" after the flying surrey.

The sudden movement of the girl had caused one of the parcels to become unwrapped, and something limp and black fell from it into the road. The tramp picked it up, and found it to be a new black silk stocking, long and fine and slender. It crunched crisply, and yet with a luxurious softness, between his fingers.

"Ther bloomin' little skeezicks!" said Whistling Dick, with a broad grin bisecting his freckled face. "W'ot do yer think of dat, now! Mer-ry Chris-mus! Sounded like a cuckoo clock, dat's what she did. Dem guys is swells, too, betcher life, an' der old 'un stacks dem sacks of dough down under his trotters like dey was common as dried apples. Been shoppin' fer Chrismus, and de kid's lost one of her new socks w'ot she was goin' to hold up Santy wid. De bloomin' little skeezicks! Wit' her 'Mer-ry Chris-mus!' W'ot d'yer t'ink! Same as to say, 'Hello, Jack, how goes it?' and as swell as Fif' Av'noo, and as easy as a blowout in Cincinnat."

Whistling Dick folded the stocking carefully and stuffed it into his pocket.

It was nearly two hours later when he came upon signs of habitation. The buildings of an extensive plantation were brought into view by a turn in the road. He easily selected the planter's residence in a large square building with two wings, with numerous good-sized, well-lighted windows, and broad verandas running around its full extent. It was set upon a smooth lawn, which was faintly lit by the far-reaching rays of the lamps within. A noble grove surrounded it, and old-fashioned shrubbery grew thickly about the walks and fences. The quarters of the hands and the mill buildings were situated at a distance in the rear.

The road was now enclosed on each side by a fence, and presently, as Whistling Dick drew nearer the houses, he suddenly stopped and sniffed the air.

"If dere ain't a hobo stew cookin' somewhere in dis immediate precinct," he said to himself, "me nose has quit tellin' de trut'."

Without hesitation he climbed the fence to windward. He found himself in an apparently disused lot, where piles of old bricks were stacked, and rejected, decaying lumber. In a corner he saw the faint glow of a fire that had become little more than a bed of living coals, and he thought he could see some dim human forms sitting or lying about it. He drew nearer, and by the light of a little blaze that suddenly flared up he saw plainly the fat figure of a ragged man in an old brown sweater and cap.

"Dat man," said Whistling Dick to himself softly, "is a dead ringer for Boston Harry. I'll try him wit de high sign."

He whistled one or two bars of a rag-time melody, and the air was immediately taken up, and then quickly ended with a peculiar run. The first whistler walked confidently up to the fire. The fat man looked up, and spake in a loud, asthmatic wheeze:

"Gents, the unexpected, but welcome, addition to our circle is Mr. Whistling Dick, an old friend of mine for whom I fully vouches.

The waiter will lay another cover at once. Mr. W. D. will join us at supper, during which function he will enlighten us in regard to the circumstances that give us the pleasure of his company."

"Chewin' de stuffin' out'n de dictionary, as usual, Boston," said Whistling Dick; "but t'anks all de same for de invitashun. I guess I finds meself here about de same way as yous guys. A cop gimme de tip dis mornin'. Yous workin' on dis farm?"

"A guest," said Boston sternly, "shouldn't never insult his entertainers until he's filled up wid grub. 'Taint good business sense. Workin'!—but I will restrain myself. We five—me, Deaf Pete, Blinky, Goggles, and Indiana Tom—got put onto this scheme of Noo Orleans to work visiting gentlemen upon her dirty streets, and we hit the road last evening just as the tender hues of twilight had flopped down upon the daisies and things. Blinky, pass the empty oyster-can at your left to the empty gentleman at your right."

For the next ten minutes the gang of roadsters paid their undivided attention to the supper. In an old five-gallon kerosene can they had cooked a stew of potatoes, meat, and onions, which they partook of from smaller cans they had found scattered about the vacant lot.

Whistling Dick had known Boston Harry of old, and knew him to be one of the shrewdest and most successful of his brotherhood. He looked like a prosperous stockdrover or a solid merchant from some country village. He was stout and hale, with a ruddy, always smoothly shaven face. His clothes were strong and neat, and he gave special attention to the care of his decent-appearing shoes. During the past ten years he had acquired a record for working a larger number of successfully managed confidence games than any of his acquaintances, and he had not a day's work to be counted against him. It was rumored among his associates that he had saved a considerable amount of money. The four other men were fair specimens of the slinking, ill-clad, noisome genus who carry their labels of "suspicious" in plain view.

After the bottom of the large can had been scraped, and pipes lit at the coals, two of the men called Boston aside and spake with him lowly and mysteriously. He nodded decisively, and then said aloud to Whistling Dick:

"Listen, sonny, to some plain talky-talk. We five are on a lay. I've guaranteed you to be square, and you're to come in on the profits equal with the boys, and you've got to help. Two hundred hands on this plantation are expecting to be paid a week's wages tomorrow morning. To-morrow's Christmas, and they want to lay off. Says the boss: 'Work from five to nine in the morning to get a train load of sugar off, and I'll pay every man cash down for the week, and a day extra.' They say: 'Hooray for the boss! It goes.' He drives to Noo Orleans to-day, and fetches back the cold dollars. Two thousand and seventy-four fifty is the amount. I got the figures from a man who talks too much, who got 'em from the book-keeper. The boss of this plantation thinks he's going to pay this wealth to the hands. He's got it down wrong; he's going to pay it to us. It's going to stay in the leisure class, where it belongs. Now, half of this haul goes to me, and the other half the rest of you may divide. Why the difference? I represent brains. It's my scheme. Here's the way we're going to get it. There's some company at supper in the house, but they'll leave about nine. They've just happened in for an hour or so. If they don't go pretty soon, we'll work the scheme anyhow. We want all night to get away good with the dollars. They're heavy. About nine o'clock Deaf Pete and Blinky'll go down the road about a quarter beyond the house, and set fire to a big cane-field there that the cutters haven't touched yet. The wind's just right to have it roaring in two minutes. The alarm'll be given, and every man Jack about the place will be down there in ten minutes, fighting fire. That'll leave the money sacks and the women alone in the house for us to handle. You've heard cane burn? Well, there's mighty few women can screech loud enough to be heard above its crackling. The thing's dead safe. The only danger is in being caught before we can get far enough away with the money. Now, if you—"

"Boston," interrupted Whistling Dick, rising to his feet, 't'anks for de grub yous fellers has give me, but I'll be movin' on now."

"What do you mean?" asked Boston, also rising.

"W'y you can count me outer dis deal. You outer know dat. I'm on de bum all right enough, but dat other t'ing don't go wit' me. Burglary is no good. I'll say good-night and many t'anks fer—"

Whistling Dick had moved away a few steps as he spoke, but he stopped very suddenly. Boston had covered him with a short revolver of roomy caliber.

"Take your seat," said the tramp leader. "I'd feel mighty proud of myself if I let you go and spoil the game. You'll stick right in this camp until we finish the job. The end of that brick pile is your limit. You go two inches beyond that, and I'll have to shoot. Better take it easy, now."

"It's my way of doin'," said Whistling Dick. "Easy goes. You can depress de muzzle of dat twelve-incher, and run 'er back on the trucks. I remains, as de newspape's says, 'in yer midst'."

"All right," said Boston, lowering his piece, as the other returned and took his seat again on a projecting plank in a pile of timber. "Don't try to leave; that's all. I wouldn't miss this chance even if I had to shoot an old acquaintance to make it go. I don't want to hurt anybody specially, but this thousand dollars I'm going to get will fix me for fair. I'm going to drop the road, and start a saloon in a little town I know about. I'm tired of being kicked around."

Boston Harry took from his pocket a cheap silver watch, and held it near the fire.

"It's a quarter to nine," he said. "Pete, you and Blinky start. Go down the road past the house, and fire the cane in a dozen places. Then strike for the levee, and come back on it, instead of the road, so you wont meet anybody. By the time you get back the men will all be striking out for the fire, and we'll break for the house and collar the dollars. Everybody cough up what matches he's got."

The two surly tramps made a collection of all the matches in the party, Whistling Dick contributing his quota with propitiatory alacrity, and then they departed in the dim starlight in the direction of the road.

Of the three remaining vagrants, two, Goggles and Indiana Tom, reclined lazily upon convenient lumber and regarded Whistling Dick with undisguised disfavor. Boston, observing that the dissenting recruit was disposed to remain peaceably, relaxed a little in his vigilance. Whistling Dick arose presently and strolled leisurely up and down, keeping carefully within the territory assigned him.

"Dis planter chap," he said, pausing before Boston Harry, "w'ot makes yer t'ink he's got de tin in de house wit' 'im?"

"I'm advised of the facts in the case," said Boston. "He drove to Noo Orleans and got it, I say, to-day. Want to change your mind and come in?"

"Naw, I was just askin'. Wot kind o' team did de boss drive?"

"Pair of grays."

"Double surrey?"

"Yep."

"Women folks along?"

"Wife and kid. Say, what morning paper are you trying to pump news for?"

"I was just conversin' to pass de time away. I guess dat team passed me in de road dis evenin'. Dat's all."

As Whistling Dick put his hands into his pockets and continued his curtailed beat up and down by the fire, he felt the silk stocking he had picked up in the road.

"Ther bloomin' little skeezicks!" he muttered, with a grin.

As he walked up and down he could see, through a sort of natural opening or lane among the trees, the planter's residence some two hundred yards distant. The side of the house toward him exhibited spacious, well-lighted windows through which a soft radiance streamed, illuminating the broad veranda and some extent of the lawn beneath.

"What's that you said?" asked Boston, sharply.

"Oh, nuttin' 't all," said Whistling Dick, lounging carelessly, and kicking meditatively at a little stone on the ground.

"Just as easy," continued the warbling vagrant softly to himself, "an' sociable an' swell an' sassy, wit' her 'Mer-ry Chris-mus,'—wot d'yer t'ink, now!"

Dinner, three hours late, was being served in the Bellemeade plantation dining-room. The dining-room and all its appurtenances spoke of an old *régime* that was here continued rather than suggested to the memory. The plate was rich to the extent that its age and quaintness alone saved it from being showy; there were interesting names signed in the corners of the pictures on the walls; the viands were of the kind that bring a shine into the eyes of *gourmets*. The service was swift, silent, lavish, as in the days when the waiters were assets like the plate. The names by which the planter's family and their visitors addressed one another were historic in the annals of two nations. Their manners and conversation had that most difficult kind of ease-the kind that still preserves punctilio. The planter himself seemed to be the dynamo that generated the larger portion of the gayety and wit. The younger ones at the board found it more than difficult to turn back upon him his guns of raillery and banter. It is true, the young men attempted to storm his works repeatedly, incited by the hope of gaining the approbation of their fair companions; but even when they sped a well-aimed shaft, the planter forced them to feel defeat by the tremendous discomfiting thunder of the laughter with which he accompanied his retorts. At the head of the table, serene, matronly, benevolent, reigned the mistress of the house, placing here and there the right smile, the right word, the encouraging glance.

The talk of the party was too desultory, too evanescent to follow, but at last they came to the subject of the tramp nuisance, one that had of late vexed the plantations for many miles around. The planter seized the occasion to direct his good-natured fire of raillery at the mistress, accusing her of encouraging the plague. "They swarm up and down the river every winter," he said. "They overrun

New Orléans, and we catch the surplus, which is generally the worst part. And, a day or two ago, Madame Nouveau Orleans, suddenly discovering that she can't go shopping without brushing her skirts against great rows of the vagabonds sunning themselves on the banquettes, says to the police: 'Catch 'em all,' and the police catch a dozen or two, and the remaining three or four thousand overflow up and down the levees, and Madame there"—pointing tragically with the carving-knife at her—"feeds them. They won't work; they defy my overseers, and they make friends with my dogs; and you, Madame, feed them before my eyes, and intimidate me when I would interfere. Tell us, please, how many to-day did you thus incite to future laziness and depredation?"

"Six, I think," said Madame, with a reflective smile; "but you know two of them offered to work, for you heard them yourself."

The planter's disconcerting laugh rang out again.

"Yes, at their own trades. And one was an artificial-flower-maker, and the other was a glass-blower. Oh, they were looking for work! Not a hand would they consent to lift to labor of any other kind."

"And another one," continued the soft-hearted mistress, "used quite good language. It was really extraordinary for one of his class. And he carried a watch. And had lived in Boston. I don't believe they are all bad. They have always seemed to me to rather lack development. I always look upon them as children with whom wisdom has remained at a standstill while dirt and whiskers have continued to grow. We passed one this evening as we were driving home who had a face as good as it was incompetent. He was whistling the intermezzo from 'Cavalleria,' and blowing the spirit of Mascagni himself into it."

A bright-eyed young girl who sat at the left of the mistress leaned over, and said in a confidential undertone:

"I wonder, mamma, if that tramp we passed on the road found my stocking, and do you think he will hang it up to-night? Now I can hang up but one. Do you know why I wanted a new pair of silk stockings when I have plenty? Well, old Aunt Judy says, if you hang up two that have never been worn, Santa Claus will fill one with good things, and Monsieur Pambé will place in the other payment for all the words you have spoken—good or bad—on the day before Christmas. That's why I've been unusually nice and polite to every one to-day. Monsieur Pambé, you know, is a witch gentleman; he—"

The words of the young girl were interrupted by a startling thing.

Like the wraith of some burned-out shooting star, a black streak came crashing through the window-pane upon the table, where it shivered into fragments a dozen pieces of crystal and china ware, and then glanced between the heads of the guests to the wall, imprinting therein a deep, round indentation, at which, to-day, the visitor to Bellemeade marvels as he gazes upon it and listens to this tale as it is told.

The women screamed in many keys, and the men sprang to their feet, and would have laid their hands upon their swords had not the verities of chronology forbidden.

The planter was the first to act; he sprang to the intruding missile, and held it up to view.

"By Jupiter!" he cried. "A meteoric shower of hosiery! Has communication at last been established with Mars?"

"I should say—ahem!—Venus," ventured a young gentleman visitor, looking hopefully for approbation toward the unresponsive young lady visitors.

The planter held at arm's length the unceremonious visitor—a long, dangling, black stocking. "She's loaded," he announced.

As he spoke he reversed the stocking, holding it by the toe, and down from it dropped a roundish stone, wrapped about by a piece of yellowish paper. "Now for the first interstellar message of the century," he cried; and nodding to the company, who had crowded about him, he adjusted his glasses with provoking deliberation, and examined it closely. When he finished, he had changed from the jolly host to the practical, decisive man of business. He immediately struck a bell, and said to the silent-footed mulatto man who responded: "Go and tell Mr. Wesley to get Reeves and Maurice and about ten stout hands they can rely upon, and come to the hall door at once. Tell him to have the men arm themselves, and bring plenty of ropes and plow lines. Tell him to hurry." And then he read aloud from the paper these words:

To The Gent of De Hous.

Dere is 5 tuff hobose xcept meself in de vaken lot near de rode war de old brick piles is. Dey got me stuck up wid a gun see and I takes dis means of comunikaten. 2 of der lads is gone down to set fire to de cain field below de hous and when yous fellers goes to turn de hoes on it de hole gang is goin to rob de hous of de money yoo got to pay off wit say git a move on ye say de kid dropt dis sock in der rode tel her mery crismus de same as she told me. Ketch de bums down de rode first and den sen a relefe core to get me out of soke yores truly

Whistlen Dick.

There was some quiet, but rapid, manceuvering at Bellemeade during the ensuing half hour, which ended in five disgusted and sullen tramps being captured, and locked securely in an outhouse pending the coming of the morning and retribution. For another result, the visiting young gentlemen had secured the unqualified worship of the visiting young ladies by their distinguished and heroic conduct. For still another, behold Whistling Dick, the hero, seated at the planter's table, feasting upon viands his experience had never before included, and waited upon by admiring feminimty in shapes of such beauty and "swellness" that even his ever-full mouth could scarcely prevent him from whistling. He was made to disclose in detail his adventure with the evil gang of Boston Harry, and how he cunningly wrote the note and wrapped it around the stone and placed it in the toe of the stocking, and, watching his chance, sent it silently, with a wonderful centrifugal momentum, like a comet, at one of the big lighted windows of the dining-room.

The planter vowed that the wanderer should wander no more; that his was a goodness and an honesty that should be rewarded, and that a debt of gratitude had been made that must be paid; for had he not saved them from a doubtless imminent loss, and, maybe, a greater calamity? He assured Whistling Dick that he might consider himself a charge upon the honor of Bellemeade; that a position suited to his powers would be found for him at once, and hinted that the way would be heartily smoothed for him to rise to as high places of emolument and trust as the plantation afforded.

But now, they said, he must be weary, and the immediate thing to consider was rest and sleep. So the mistress spoke to a servant, and Whistling Dick was conducted to a room in the wing of the house occupied by the servants. To this room, in a few minutes, was brought a portable tin bathtub filled with water, which was placed on a piece of oiled cloth upon the floor. Here the vagrant was left to pass the night.

By the light of a candle he examined the room. A bed, with the covers neatly turned back, revealed snowy pillows and sheets. A worn, but clean, red carpet covered the floor. There was a dresser with a beveled mirror, a washstand with a flowered bowl and pitchers; the two or three chairs were softly upholstered. A little table held books, paper, and a day-old cluster of roses in a jar. There were towels on a rack and soap in a white dish.

Whistling Dick set his candle on a chair, and placed his hat carefully under the table. After satisfying what we must suppose to have been his curiosity by a sober scrutiny, he removed his coat, folded it, and laid it upon the floor, near the wall, as far as possible from the unused bathtub. Taking his coat for a pillow, he stretched himself luxuriously upon the carpet.

The tale of the historian is often disappointing; and if the historian be a workman who has an eye for effect and proportion, he has temptations to inaccuracy. For results fail to adjust themselves logically, and evince the most profound indifference toward artistic

consequence. But here we are at the mercy of facts, and the uni-
ties—whatever they may be—must be crushed beneath an impo-
tent conclusion.

When, on Christmas morning, the first streaks of dawn broke
above the marshes, Whistling Dick awoke, and reached instinc-
tively for his hat. Then he remembered that the skirts of Fortune
had swept him into their folds on the night previous, and he went to
the window and raised it, to let the fresh breath of the morning cool
his brow and fix the yet dream-like memory of his good luck within
his brain.

As he stood there, certain dread and ominous sounds pierced
the fearful hollow of his ear.

The force of plantation workers, eager to complete the short-
ened task allotted them, were all astir. The mighty din of the ogre
Labor shook the earth, and the poor tattered and forever disguised
Prince in Search of his Fortune held tight to the window sill even in
the enchanted castle, and trembled.

Already from the bosom of the mill came the thunder of rolling
barrels of sugar, and (prison-like sound) there was a great rattling of
chains as the mules were harried with stimulant imprecations to
their places by wagon tongues. A little vicious "dummy" engine,
with a train of flat cars in tow, stewed and fumed on the plantation
tap of the narrow-gauge railroad, and a toiling, hurrying, halloing
stream of workers were dimly seen in the half darkness loading the
train with the weekly output of sugar. Here was a poem; an epic—
nay, a tragedy—with Work! the curse of the world, for its theme.

The December air was frosty, but the sweat broke out upon
Whistling Dick's face. He thrust his head out of the window, and
looked down. Fifteen feet below him, against the wall of the house,
he could make out that a border of flowers grew, and by that token
he overhung a bed of soft earth.

Softly as a burglar goes, he clambered out upon the sill, lowered himself until he hung by his hands alone, and then dropped
safely. No one seemed to be about upon this side of the house. He

dodged low, and skimmed swiftly across the yard to the low fence. It was an easy matter to vault this, for a terror urged him such as lifts the gazelle over the thorn bush when the lion pursues. A crush through the dew-drenched weeds on the roadside, a clutching, slippery rush up the grassy side of the levee to the footpath at the summit, and—he was free!

The east was blushing and brightening. The wind, himself a vagrant rover, saluted his brother upon the cheek. Some wild geese, high above, gave cry. A rabbit skipped along the path before him, free to turn to the right or to the left as his mood should send him. The river slid past, and certainly no one could tell the ultimate abiding place of its waters.

A small, ruffled, brown-breasted bird, sitting upon a dogwood sapling, began a soft, throaty, tender little piping in praise of the dew which entices foolish worms from their holes; but suddenly he stopped, and sat with his head turned sidewise, listening.

From the path along the levee there burst forth a jubilant, stirring, buoyant, thrilling whistle, loud and keen and clear as the cleanest notes of the piccolo. The soaring sound rippled and trilled and arpeggioed as the songs of wild birds do not; but it had a wild free grace that, in a way, reminded the small brown bird of something familiar, but exactly what he could not tell. There was in it the bird call, or reveille, that all birds know; but a great waste of lavish, unmeaning things that art had added and arranged, besides, and that were quite puzzling and strange; and the little brown bird sat with his head on one side until the sound died away in the distance.

The little bird did not know that the part of that strange warbling that he understood was just what kept the warbler without his breakfast that morning; but he knew very well that the part he did not understand did not concern him, so he gave a little flutter of his wings and swooped down like a brown bullet upon a big fat worm that was wriggling on the levee path.

A Plantation Christmas

JULIA PETERKIN
(1880–1961)

Julia Peterkin was born Julia Mood in Laurens County, South
Carolina, where her father was a prominent country doctor. She
graduated from Converse College in 1896 and accepted a position teaching in a one-room school in the Low Country town of
Fort Motte, South Carolina. In 1903 she married William
Peterkin, owner of the Lang Syne Plantation. Julia Peterkin
assumed managerial duties of the large plantation, responsibili-
ties that she would shoulder for life. She gained an understanding of the life and folk-ways of the Gullahs who worked on the
plantation and wrote honestly of their practices in her fiction.
Peterkin's first sketches were published in the early 1920s, first in
H.L. Mencken's *Smart Set*, then in Emily Clark's *Reviewer*. Her
first book, *Green Thursday* (1924), was a collection of *Reviewer*
sketches strung together by a narrative. Peterkin's novel *Black
April* (1927) was followed by *Scarlet Sister Mary* (1929) for which
she won the Pulitzer Prize in fiction. Her books realistically portrayed the blacks of her region, and Peterkin said, "I mean to present these people in a patient struggle with fate," and "do them as
they really are." After the success of *Scarlet Sister Mary*, Peterkin
published *Bright Skin* (1932), a novel, *Roll, Jordan, Roll* (1933),
a nonfiction work with photographs by Doris Ullman, and *A
Plantation Christmas* (1934). Originally published in *Country
Gentleman* in 1929, *A Plantation Christmas* is Peterkin's celebration of "the miracle we call life."

I hear that in many places something has happened to
Christmas; that it is changing from a time of merriment and
carefree gaiety to a holiday that is filled with tedium; that
many people dread the day and the obligation to give Christmas
presents is nightmare to weary bored souls; that the children of is by

enlightened parents no longer believe in Santa Claus; that all in all, the effort to be happy and have pleasure makes many honest hearts grow dark with despair instead of beaming with good will and cheerfulness.

These dark rumors make me thank the kind fate which has placed me in a home which is removed from the beaten track of that thing which, for want of a better name, we call progress. Here, where time moves slowly and few changes come in, we remain faithful to the old-fashioned ways which were a part of our childhood and the childhood of those who were here before us, and we delight in defending them against anything which tends to destroy them or to lessen their brightness.

Every manner of life has its compensations, but nowhere is life more generous in compensating for its lacks than on this old plantation.

Individuals are few, so each one counts for much. Hours are long and quiet time in abundant. Since loneliness is one of the evils which threaten us, our holidays are important occasions. Birthdays, anniversaries, old church festivals, long forgotten by most of the outside world, make reasons for us to gather our friends together and make merry. But among all these gala days Christmas comes first. Our Christmas preparations begin as soon as Thanksgiving is over, when the Christmas cakes are baked and put away to ripen, with oiled paper wrapped carefully around them to hold the delicious flavor of the scuppernong wine which has been carefully poured all over their dark brown crusts.

The house servants begin to bestir themselves industriously in order to have every piece of glass and silver bright and shining, every piece of furniture and every floor polished and looking its best.

The pantry shelves already hold rows of jars filled with jellies and jams and pickles and preserves made of figs and peaches and apples and watermelon rinds, and every other fruit and vegetable the garden and orchard yield. Bottles of red and white juices made of berries and grapes stand in colorful and tempting array until they are ready to be used.

In the kitchen, the cook moves about with much dignity and importance among his pots and pans and measuring-cups and scales, pausing now and then to ponder over some old recipe stored away in his mind or to boast of how much better he can cook out of his head than most people can cook out of books.

Long strands of red peppers hang to nails outside the kitchen door, ready to season the Christmas turkey dressing. Store-bought pepper is hot enough, but it lacks the flavor which theses home-grown peppers give, not only to the turkey dressing and the game which hunters bring in, but to the links of sausage which will soon be strung across the smokehouse and piles of rich liver pudding in which rice and corn meal both furnish such a large share.

The shoats are growing fatter each day on the sweet acorns falling from live-ok trees, and on the peanuts and potatoes, peas and ears of corn which were left in the fields when those crops were gathered.

In the wild-crabapple thickets of fruit is covering the ground, for nights are cool and frosty; enough must be gathered for the clear yellow bitter-sweet jelly which is perfect with roasted pork hams.

The sugar-cane mills scattered over the place cannot finish all their work by daylight and their bright fires make shining red stars are night, while the fragrance of the boiling sirup steams up from the brown gallons which simmer and thicken in the wood-lined vats, promising molasses cake and delicious candy and the best sirup that was ever poured over hot waffles.

The sweet potatoes are in banks, the hay is in stacks, the corn is in the barns, most of the cotton has been picked. Still, the cotton-pickers sing and laugh and talk happily as they pick the last scatter-ing white locks out of belated bolls, for every extra pound of cotton means extra coins for Christmas, and at Christmas-time money is needed, not only for necessities, but for pleasuring.

The cotton gins tun at full tilt, packing the last cotton into bales while the plantation foreman, big, black, muscular, keen-eyed, walks about among the belts and pulleys and running gear, watching the soft white downy streams pour our from the gin rolls into press to be packed and then labeled with the owner's mark.

Axes swing and ring in the woods nearby as their sharp steel is driven into the hearts of trees. As the fresh logs are cut, they are hauled in, and woodpiles grow high in every backyard. A clean hickory backlog for the Christmas fire lies waiting on every pile beside the sturdy lengths of pine and oak and ash, and the fat rosiny pine knots and bits of pine hearts are spilt up into small kindling wood which can rouse the sleepiest blaze into bright burning.

The wild broom grass, with its tall strong growth, is ripe enough to gather, and the year's supply of brooms must be wrung before a hard frost comes and scorches the straw and makes it lifeless and brittle. Bound into neat bundles with withes of split hickory so that they can make a comfortable handful, these brooms make welcome Christmas presents. No store-bought broom can sweep dust out of corners half so well.

Partridges like broom fields, and it is not uncommon for fine coveys to flutter up and away with startling whirs, or for rabbits to go bouncing through the sedge at the sight of the broom-gatherers who wring the straw.

The old houses in the Quarters have been weathered by long years of rain and wind and sunshine into a soft gray, but underneath this gentle color their yellow wood stands as solid and steadfast as it was a hundred years ago.

Before Christmas Eve the old cypress floors must be scoured white, inside walls repapered with newspapers pasted on tight, the mantle-shelves and bare rafters decorated with papers cut into fringes and scallops. The front doors and window blinds must be whitewashed with lime or with white clay which lines the big gully near the spring. The yards must be raked and swept clean, for everything must be spick-and-span and neat for Christmas.

The store at the crossroads is kept open until long after dark, for the buying for Christmas must be carefully done, and those who come to buy like to linger and talk awhile. Printed words are scarce and so spoken words are all the more precious. News has to be passed on, old tales retold, present problems discussed and measured by old-fashioned wisdom. For old fashions are still in style here. Age has precedence, children are trained to be seen and not heard, and they are expected to listen quietly while their elders repeat their tales of days which are forever gone, but which have left so many fine old beliefs and traditions.

Everybody goes dressed in his Sunday best, and merry laughter rises above the serious words of buying. Friendly hands are shaken and held. Treats are offered and accepted graciously.

Glass bottles with string tied around their necks for handles gurgle as they are filled with kerosene. Paper bags threaten to burst and spill loads of fruit and candy and cakes they are given to hold. The scent of coffee newly parched and ground smothers the pleasant smell of the bunches of bananas which swing from the ceiling and the rank scent of dried herrings in their stained slatted boxes.

The gristmill across the road clatters noisily as it grinds hoppers full of corn into meal and hominy, and the miller's black hands and eyebrows are whitened with the soft dust as he rubs the crushed grain between his fingers to see if its fineness is right.

The restaurant next door flaps its red-and-white calico curtains and sends out inviting odors of catfish and rice.

In a pit at one side of the restaurant's yard, a barbecued pig drips sizzling fat on the coals which have cooked it so done and brown. Barbecue sandwiches are made of pork and slices of store-bought bread rival the catfish and rice as a welcome change from the food eaten every day. Gallant beaus escort their ladies about and feed them well. Banjos and guitars plucked by work-hardened fingers add music and encourage the singing and dancing.

Many strange styles of dress are seen. The middle-aged and elderly women keep to their old-time full, long skirts, which are usually half-hidden by wide white aprons, and their heads are neatly tied with bandanna headkerchiefs, large squares of white cambric or black calico which are bound gracefully around their heads and tied with a deft knot in the back. No head covering could be more dignified or becoming than these kerchiefs, especially when another square of the same material is folded around the wearer's neck and pinned across her bosom.

Bright hoop earrings twinkle in many ears, for they make the wearer's eyesight better; strings of gay beads tinkle around many necks, setting off the holiday costumes.

Christmas is no holiday gotten up for the amusement of children, but a season which is enjoyed by the grown people with utmost enthusiasm. People who have always loved one another are bound closer by the fun they have together. Old pain and old strain are forgotten in the good time which is come. There is a sudden new joy in just being alive.

Important journeys are made to town, where the matter of choosing Christmas presents becomes so absorbing that traffic lights are overlooked and remembered only when indignant traffic cops shout severe reprimands.

If we lived nearer to many stores and were used to getting packages, then the pleasure of sending and receiving gifts might be less. If the circle of our friends was larger, the sheer fun of deciding what each one would like might not be so great. But here the mere sight of an acquaintance warms our hearts, and just knowing that the sight of ourselves makes other hearts glad is one of life's richest experiences.

Fine mornings are spent getting Christmas trees from the woods, in making holly wreaths and hanging up mistletoe boughs. The days are golden with sunshine, the forests glowing with color. Everywhere there is fulfillment of last spring's promise. Black walnuts and hickory buts drop with empathic thuds; chinquapins fall from dry burs and hide under their own fallen leaves; under live-oaks, water-oaks, Spanish oaks, the earth is covered with acorns, yet the chestnut-oaks drop their loads of big over-cups in a steady patter.

The magnolias are green and glossy, mock oranges glisten in the sunlight, Cherokee-rose apples shine among the glossy leaves.

Sometimes Autumn is generous and lets some of its blossoms stay until Christmas. Roses bloom, chrysanthemums are bewilderingly brilliant in a few protected places, Cape jasmines linger to help the tea olives keep the air perfumed, and vagrant butterflies hover the frost-tinged zinnias and marigolds.

A festival without feasting would be an empty thing, and the hunters all go out for game. Doves and partridges are plentiful, the big wild ducks have come to spend the winter in the swamps where the sweet gums, drunk on the warmth of the mild winter sunshine, scatter leaves in bright showers of purple and gold with every stir of the wind, hiding the deer tracks which mingle with those of turkeys and wildcats and foxes and raccoons.

The mazes of the swamp are treacherous, but one glimpse of a wild gobbler's shining, burnished feathers is enough to induce any hunter to go slipping stealthily between the great trunks of cypresses and sweet gums, climbing over fallen logs, tramping through mud, side-stepping bogs, stooping under the low-swung nooses of wild grapevines and thorny bamboos.

Christmas Eve finds the plantation rich with unexpected things. Unusual sounds and colors are everywhere. Happy voices rise above the whispering and rustling of paper wrappings, fires crackle and heighten and shed a rosy glow over the Christmas decorations and warn the outside dankness to keep away. As the first stars twinkle out, the whole world become radiant with a light which does not come from the sky, because once, long ago, the Star of Bethlehem shone just so above the manger where Jesus Christ was born. The fields lie quiet, the hills away over the river are folded with hazy blue, and the hearts of human beings beat softly because He who could heal the sick and raise the dead and make the sinful sinless was born on just such a night.

Suppers are eaten early so that the fires can be covered and the houses closed by the time the old cowbell starts ringing to tell the people that the time for watch-night meeting in the Quarters is near. Nobody wants to be late, although the meeting lasts until dawn.

The cows are left unmilked with their calves, for al creatures are alike on Christmas Eve night, and mothers, whether they are beast or women, whether they pray in churches or in stables and stalls, want their children close beside them when they kneel at midnight to pray to the great Father of us all.

Wheels creak along the roads that lead through the fields toward the Quarters, for they carry heavy loads of people. The old meeting benches sag with the weight of so many who have come to worship. Heads are bowed and glad tears are shed as the story of the first Christmas is read from the Book, and Christians are reminded that the sky holds a resting-place for them, that in Heaven many mansions have room for all who need peace and comfort.

Solemn, soul-stirring old hymns, lined out two lines at a time in the deep, booming voice of the prayer leader, are sung until midnight, and prayers lifted high by earnest, reverent voices pleading with the Most High for His blessing and protection rise and fall like breakers on the beach. But as soon as the cocks crow to announce that middle-night, the holy hour, has come, then the prayers change into rejoicing. The old meeting-house walls ring with exultant voices, the old floor boards give them the beating of so many shouting feet. All night long singing voices float out into the darkness and join blurred songs of the wind in the trees until the morning star rides high in the sky and the Christmas sun rises shouting in the east. Then the benediction is said.

The cock crowing for sunrise is scarcely over when the servants steal into the Big House on tiptoe so they can catch everybody there with a shouted 'Christmas Gift!' before the kitchen fire is even started or the water put on to boil for the early morning coffee.

This is an old game. Everybody tries to catch everybody else and win an extra Christmas gift. Kind old maumas arrive before breakfast is over, fetching presents of new-laid eggs or fat pullet chickens tied by the legs, and their thanks for their gifts—aprons or sweets or fruits, or whatever else has been prepared for them—are expressed in the most charming, gracious words accompanied by the most graceful curtsies. Gentle old men fetch bags of peanuts or ears of popcorn or bottles of homemade sirup.

The cook forgets the heavy day's work ahead of him and joins heartily in the singing of Christmas spirituals out in the yard. The words of the beautiful songs are few, but their refrains repeated over and over in a thundering swirl unite us all in voice and faith and joy and help us to know that Christmas Day is the best day of our year.

And Christmas Week is our best week. Every night the big drum booms out with an invitation to a Christmas-tree party at some cabin. The Big House at the neighboring plantations are filled with fun until New Year's Day comes and ends the glad holiday season.

When nothing is left of the merry-making but withered holly and faded mistletoe and the few red embers that still shine among the hickory ashes of the Christmas backlog, we rejoice that we are spared to pause and wonder over that strange miracle we call life.

On Christmas Eve

LANGSTON HUGHES
(1902–1967)

Langston Hughes was born in Joplin, Missouri, but spent much of his childhood with his grandmother in Lawrence, Kansas after the separation of his parents. His mother took him to plays and readings, and Hughes recalled his grandmother telling him stories. After the death of his grandmother in 1916, Hughes lived with his mother in Lincoln, Illinois, where he published several poems in his high school's literary magazine. In 1920, he journeyed to Mexico to live with his father and during this time published his first work of prose, "Mexican Games" in the NAACP's children's magazine, *Brownie's Book*. The editors of another NAACP magazine, *Crisis*, published "The Negro Speaks of Rivers" (1921), which became one of his best known poems. Hughes attended Columbia University for one year, and then led a vagabond existence for several years. He worked odd jobs in New York City and served as a ship's mess boy, which allowed him to travel to Africa and Europe. While working as a bus boy at the Wardman Park hotel in Washington, D.C., he met Vachel Lindsay, who encouraged him in his writing and brought him to the attention of the media, calling him the "bus boy poet." He then attended Lincoln University and published his first book of poems, *The Weary Blues* (1926), which brought him critical acclaim. Hughes became a major figure in the Harlem Renaissance and in 1926 defined his mission as an artist, "to write about the black man in America with truth and honesty." Hughes went on a poetry-reading tour of the South in 1931 and 1932, where he met Margaret Walker. Hughes also enjoyed success as a humorist, novelist, and playwright, and in 1938 founded the Harlem Suitcase Theatre. At the time of his death, Hughes had written, edited and translated over sixty books. The following story, "One Christmas Eve," is a selection from *The Ways of White Folks* (1934).

⊤

Standing over the hot stove cooking supper, the colored maid, Arcie, was very tired. Between meals today, she had cleaned the whole house for the white family she worked for, getting ready for Christmas tomorrow. Now her back ached and her head felt faint from sheer fatigue. Well, she would be off in a little while, if only the Missus and her children would come on home to dinner. They were out shopping for more things for the tree which stood all ready, tinsel-hung and lovely in the living-room, waiting for its candles to be lighted.

Arcie wished she could afford a tree for Joe. He'd never had one yet, and it's nice to have such things when you're little. Joe was five, going on six. Arcie, looking at the roast in the white folks' oven, wondered how much she could afford to spend tonight on toys. She only got seven dollars a week, and four of that went for her room and the landlady's daily looking after Joe while Arcie was at work.

"Lord, it's more'n a notion raisin' a child," she thought.

She looked at the clock on the kitchen table. After seven. What made white folks so darned inconsiderate? Why didn't they come on home here to supper? They knew she wanted to get off before all the stores closed. She wouldn't have time to buy Joe nothin' if they didn't hurry. And her landlady probably wanting to go out and shop, too, and not be bothered with little Joe.

"Dog gone it!" Arcie said to herself "If I just had my money, I might leave the supper on the stove for 'em. I just got to get to the stores fo' they close." But she hadn't been paid for the week yet. The Missus had promised to pay her Christmas Eve, a day or so ahead of time.

Arcie heard a door slam and talking and laughter in the front of the house. She went in and saw the Missus and her kids shaking snow off their coats.

"Ummm-mm! It's swell for Christmas Eve," one of the kids said to Arcie. "It's snowin' like the deuce, and mother came near driving through a stop light. Can't hardly see for the snow. It's swell!"

"Supper's ready," Arcie said. She was thinking how her shoes weren't very good for walking in snow.

It seemed like the white folks took as long as they could to eat that evening. While Arcie was washing dishes, the Missus came out with her money.

"Arcie," the Missus said, 'I'm so sorry, but would you mind if I just gave you five dollars tonight? The children have made me run short of change, buying presents and all.

"I'd like to have seven," Arcie said. "I needs it."

"Well, I just haven't got seven," the Missus said. "I didn't know you'd want all your money before the end of the week, anyhow. I just haven't got it to spare."

Arcie took five. Coming out of the hot kitchen, she wrapped up as well as she could and hurried by the house where she roomed to get little Joe. At least he could look at the Christmas trees in the windows downtown.

The landlady, a big light yellow woman, was in a bad humor. She said to Arcie, "I thought you was comm' home early and get this child. I guess you know I want to go out, too, once in awhile."

Arcie didn't say anything for, if she had, she knew the landlady would probably throw it up to her that she wasn't getting paid to look after a child both night and day.

"Come on, Joe," Arcie said to her son, "let's us go in the street."

"I hears they got a Santa Claus downtown," Joe said, wriggling into his worn little coat. "I wants to see him."

"Don't know 'bout that," his mother said, "but hurry up and get your rubbers on. Stores'll all be closed directly."

It was six or eight blocks downtown. They trudged along through the falling snow, both of them a little cold. But the snow was pretty!

The main street was hung with bright red and blue lights. In front of the City Hall there was a Christmas tree-but it didn't have no presents on it, only lights. In the store windows there were lots of toys—for sale.

Joe kept on saying, "Mama, I want. . ."

But mama kept walking ahead. It was nearly ten, when the stores were due to close, and Arcie wanted to get Joe some cheap gloves and something to keep him warm, as well as a toy or two. She thought she might come across a rummage sale where they had children's clothes. And in the ten-cent store, she could get some toys.

"O-oo! Lookee . . . ," little Joe kept saying, and pointing at things in the windows. How warm and pretty the lights were, and the shops, and the electric signs through the snow.

It took Arcie more than a dollar to get Joe's mittens and things he needed. In the A & P Arcie bought a big box of hard candies for 49$. And then she guided Joe through the crowd on the street until they came to the dime store. Near the ten-cent store they passed a moving picture theatre. Joe said he wanted to go in and see the movies.

Arcie said, "Ump-un! No, child! This ain't Baltimore where they have shows for colored, too. In these here small towns, they don't let colored folks in. We can't go in there."

"Oh," said little Joe.

In the ten-cent store, there was an awful crowd. Arcie told Joe to stand outside and wait for her. Keeping hold of him in the crowded store would be a job. Besides she didn't want him to see what toys she was buying. They were to be a surprise from Santa Claus tomorrow.

Little Joe stood outside the ten-cent store in the light, and the snow, and people passing. Gee, Christmas was pretty. All tinsel and stars and cotton. And Santa Claus a-coming from somewhere, dropping things in stockings. And all the people in the streets were carrying things, and the kids looked happy.

But Joe soon got tired of just standing and thinking and waiting in front of the ten-cent store. There were so many things to look at in the other windows. He moved along up the block a little, and then a little more, walking and looking. In fact, he moved until he came to the white folks' picture show.

In the lobby of the moving picture show, behind the plate-glass doors, it was all warm and glowing and awful pretty. Joe stood looking in, and as he looked his eyes began to make out, in there blazing beneath holly and colored streamers and the electric stars of the lobby, a marvelous Christmas tree. A group of children and grown-ups, white, of course, were standing around a big jovial man in red beside the tree. Or was it a man? Little Joe's eyes opened wide. No, it was not a man at all. It was Santa Claus!

Little Joe pushed open one of the glass doors and ran into the lobby of the white moving picture show. Little Joe went right through the crowd and up to where he could get a good look at Santa Claus. And Santa Claus was giving away gifts, little presents for children, little boxes of animal crackers and stick-candy canes. And behind him on the tree was a big sign (which little Joe didn't know how to read).It said, to those who understood, MERRY XMAS FROM SANTA CLAUS TO OUR YOUNG PATRONS.

Around the lobby, other signs said, WHEN YOU COME OUT OF THE SHOW STOP WITH YOUR CHILDREN AND SEE OUR SANTA CLAUS. And another announced, GEM THE-ATRE MAKES ITS CUSTOMERS HAPPY— SEE OUR SANTA.

And there was Santa Claus in a red suit and a white beard all sprinkled with tinsel snow. Around him were rattles and drums and rocking horses which he was not giving away. But the signs on them said (could little Joe have read) that they would be presented from the stage on Christmas Day to the holders of the lucky numbers. Tonight, Santa Claus was only giving away candy, and stick-candy canes, and animal crackers to the kids.

Joe would have liked terribly to have a stick-candy cane. He came a little closer to Santa Claus, until he was right in the front of the crowd. And then Santa Claus saw Joe.

Why is it that lots of white people always grin when they see a Negro child? Santa Claus grinned. Everybody else grinned, too, looking at little black Joe—who had no business in the lobby of a white theatre. Then Santa Claus stooped down and slyly picked up one of his lucky number rattles, a great big loud tin-pan rattle such as they use in cabarets. And he shook it fiercely right at Joe. That was funny. The white people laughed, kids and all. But little Joe didn't laugh. He was scared. To the shaking of the big rattle, he turned and fled out of the warm lobby of the theatre, out into the street where the snow was and the people. Frightened by laughter, he had begun to cry. He went looking for his mama. In his heart he never thought Santa Claus shook great rattles at children like that—and then laughed.

In the crowd on the street he went the wrong way. He couldn't find the ten-cent store or his mother. There were too many people, all white people, moving like white shadows in the snow, a world of white people.

It seemed to Joe an awfully long time till he suddenly saw Arcie, dark and worried-looking, cut across the side-walk through the passing crowd and grab him. Although her arms were full of packages, she still managed with one free hand to shake him until his teeth rattled.

"Why didn't you stand where I left you?" Arcie demanded loudly. "Tired as I am, I got to run all over the streets in the night lookin' for you. I'm a great mind to wear you out."

When little Joe got his breath back, on the way home, he told his mama he had been in the moving picture show.

"But Santa Claus didn't give me nothin'," Joe said tearfully. "He made a big noise at me and I runned out."

"Serves you right," said Arcie, trudging through the snow. "You had no business in there. I told you to stay where I left you."

"But I seed Santa Claus in there," little Joe said, "so I went in."

"Huh! That wasn't no Santa Claus," Arcie explained. "If it was, he wouldn't a-treated you like that. That's a theatre for white folks— I told you once—and he's just a old white man."

"Oh . . .," said little Joe.

from "A Christmas Story"

KATHERINE ANNE PORTER
(1890-1980)

Katherine Anne Porter, a descendent of Daniel Boone and a distant cousin to William Sydney Porter, was born Callie Russell Porter in 1890 in Indian Creek, Texas. After her mother's death in 1892, the family moved to Kyle, Texas and lived with her grandmother until her death in 1901. Following a period of dislocation, the family settled in San Antonio, where Porter attended the Thomas School to study the dramatic arts. At the age of sixteen, Porter married John Henry Koontz, a railway clerk and member of a prominent Catholic family. Callie Porter was attracted to the rituals of the church and converted to Roman Catholicism at the age of twenty, although in later years she liked to tell stories of her Catholic upbringing. Frustrated by her husband's limited prospects, Porter divorced Koontz in 1915 and moved to Chicago to pursue a career as a movie actress, assuming the name Katherine Anne Porter. Acting jobs were scarce and for the next several years Porter earned her livelihood writing book and theatre reviews for various newspapers. She also began writing poetry and short stories, and her first published story, "Maria Conception," appeared in *Century* magazine in 1922. Variously based in Chicago, Denver, New York City, and Mexico, it was Porter's time in Mexico that provided the basis of her story, "Flowering Judas," the title story of her first collection. *Flowering Judas* (1930) established Porter's literary reputation and, as a result of its success, the Guggenheim awarded her a fellowship in 1931. Porter decided to travel from Mexico to Europe, choosing the cheapest means possible, the S.S. *Werra,* what she called a "tramp steamer disguised as a passenger ship." Porter took detailed notes, immediately seeing this journey as potential for a short story, which she tentatively titled, "The Promised Land." It eventually grew into her bestselling novel, *Ship of Fools* (1962). *The Collected Stories of Katherine Anne Porter* (1965) was published to critical acclaim, winning Porter both a Pulitzer Prize and a National Book Award. In 1967, the same year Porter won a Gold Medal from the National Institute of Arts and Letters.

Seymour Lawrence, who had shepherded *Ship of Fools* to publication at the *Atlantic Monthly Press,* published *A Christmas Story,* with illustrations by Ben Shahn, under his Delacourte Press imprint. *A Christmas Story,* which Porter calls "a lament in the form of a joyous remembrance," of her niece Mary Alice, was originally published in *Mademoiselle* in 1946.

hen she was five years old, my niece asked me again why we celebrated Christmas. She had asked when she was three and when she was four, and each time had listened with a shining, believing face, learning the songs and gazing enchanted at the pictures which I displayed as proof of my stories. Nothing could have been more successful, so I began once more confidently to recite in effect the following:

The feast in the beginning was meant to celebrate with joy the birth of a Child, an event of such importance to this world that angels sang from the skies in human language to announce it and even, if we may believe the old painters, came down with garlands in their hands and danced on the broken roof of the cattle shed where He was born.

"Poor baby," she said, disregarding the angels, "didn't His papa and mama have a house?"

They weren't quite so poor as all that, I went on, slightly dashed, for last year the angels had been the center of interest. His papa and mama were able to pay taxes at least, but they had to leave home and go to Bethlehem to pay them, and they could have afforded a room at the inn, but the town was crowded because everybody came to pay taxes at the same time. They were quite lucky to find a manger full of clean straw to sleep in. When the baby was born, a goodhearted servant girl named Bertha came to help the mother. Bertha had no arms, but in that moment she unexpectedly grew a fine new pair of arms and hands, and the first thing she did with them was to wrap the baby in swaddling clothes. We then sang together the song about Bertha the armless servant. Thinking I saw a practical question dawning in a pure blue eye I hurried on to the part about how all the animals—cows, calves, donkeys, sheep —

"And pigs?"

Pigs perhaps even had knelt in a ring around the baby and breathed upon Him to keep Him warm through His first hours in this world. A new star appeared and moved in a straight course toward Bethlehem for many nights to guide three kings who came from far countries to place important gifts in the straw beside Him: gold, frankincense and myrrh.

"What beautiful clothes," said the little girl, looking at the picture of Charles the Seventh of France kneeling before a meek blond girl and a charming baby.

It was the way some people used to dress. The Child's mother, Mary, and His father, Joseph, a carpenter, were such unworldly simple souls they never once thought of taking any honor to themselves nor of turning the gifts to their own benefit.

"What became of the gifts?" asked the little girl.

Nobody knows, nobody seems to have paid much attention to them, they were never heard of again after that night. So far as we know, those were the only presents anyone ever gave to the Child while He lived. But He was not unhappy. Once He caused a cherry tree in full fruit to bend down one of its branches so His mother could more easily pick cherries. We then sang about the cherry tree until we came to the words *Then up spake old Joseph, so rude and unkind.*

"Why was he unkind?"

I thought perhaps he was just in a cross mood.

"What was he cross about?"

Dear me, what should I say now? After all, this was not *my* daughter, whatever would her mother answer to this? I asked her in turn what she was cross about when she was cross? She couldn't remember ever having been cross but was willing to let the subject pass. We moved on to *The Withy Tree*, which tells how the Child once cast a bridge of sunbeams over a stream and crossed upon it, and played a trick on little John the Baptist, who followed Him, by removing the beams and letting John fall in the water. The Child's mother switched Him smartly for this with a branch of withy, and the Child shed loud tears and wished bad luck upon the whole race of withies for ever.

"What's a withy?" asked the little girl. I looked it up in the dictionary and discovered it meant osiers, or willows.

"Just a willow like ours?" she asked, rejecting this intrusion of the commonplace. Yes, but once, when His father was struggling with a heavy piece of timber almost beyond his strength, the Child ran and touched it with one finger and the timber rose and fell properly into place. At night His mother cradled Him and sang long slow songs about a lonely tree waiting for Him in a far place; and the Child, moved by her tears, spoke long before it was time for Him to speak and His first words were, "Don't be sad, for you shall be Queen of Heaven." And there she was in an old picture, with the airy jeweled crown being set upon her golden hair.

I thought how nearly all of these tender medieval songs and legends about this Child were concerned with trees, wood, timbers, beams, cross-pieces; and even the pagan north transformed its great druidic tree festooned with human entrails into a blithe festival tree hung with gifts for the Child, and some savage old man of the woods became a rollicking saint with a big belly. But I had never talked about Santa Claus, because myself I had not liked him from the first, and did not even then approve of the boisterous way he had almost crowded out the Child from His own birthday feast.

"I like the part about the sunbeam bridge the best," said the little girl, and then she told me she had a dollar of her own and would I take her to buy a Christmas present for her mother.

We wandered from shop to shop, and I admired the way the little girl, surrounded by tons of seductive, specially manufactured holiday merchandise for children, kept her attention fixed resolutely on objects appropriate to the grown-up world. She considered seriously in turn a silver tea service, one thousand dollars; an embroidered handkerchief with lace on it, five dollars; a dressing-table mirror framed in porcelain flowers, eighty-five dollars; a preposterously showy crystal flask of perfume, one hundred twenty dollars; a gadget for curling the eyelashes, seventy-five cents; a large plaque of colored glass jewelry, thirty dollars; a cigarette case of some fraudulent material, two dollars and fifty cents. She weakened, but only for a moment, before a mechanical monkey with real fur who did calisthenics on a crossbar if you wound him up, one dollar and ninety-eight cents.

The prices of these objects did not influence their relative value to her and bore no connection whatever to the dollar she carried in her hand. Our shopping had also no connection with the birthday of the Child or the legends and pictures. Her air of reserve toward the long series of blear-eyed, shapeless old men wearing red flannel blouses and false, white-wool whiskers said all too plainly that they in no way fulfilled her notions of Christmas merriment. She shook hands with all of them politely, could not be persuaded to ask for anything from them and seemed not to question the obvious spectacle of thousands of persons everywhere buying presents instead of waiting for one of the army of Santa Clauses to bring them, as they all so profusely promised.

Christmas is what we make it and this is what we have so cynically made of it: not the feast of the Child in the straw-filled crib, nor even the homely winter bounty of the old pagan with the reindeer, but a great glittering commercial fair, gay enough with music and food and extravagance of feeling and behavior and expense, more and more on the order of the ancient Saturnalia. I have nothing against Saturnalia, it belongs to this season of the year: but how do we get so confused about the true meaning of even our simplest-appearing pastimes?

Meanwhile, for our money we found a present for the little girl's mother. It turned out to be a small green pottery shell with a colored bird perched on the rim which the little girl took for an ash tray, which it may as well have been.

"We'll wrap it up and hang it on the tree and *say* it came from Santa Claus," she said, trustfully making of me a fellow conspirator.

"You don't believe in Santa Claus any more?" I asked carefully, for we had taken her infant credulity for granted. I had already seen in her face that morning a skeptical view of my sentimental legends, she was plainly trying to sort out one thing from another in them: and I was turning over in my mind the notion of beginning again with her on other grounds, of making an attempt to draw, however faintly, some boundary lines between fact and fancy, which is not so difficult; but also further to show where truth and poetry were, if not the same being, at least twins who could wear each other's clothes. But that couldn't be done in a day nor with pedantic intention. I was perfectly prepared for the first half of her answer, but the second took me by surprise.

"No, I don't," she said, with the freedom of her natural candor, "but please don't tell my mother, for she still does." For herself, then, she rejected the gigantic hoax which a whole powerful society had organized and was sustaining at the vastest pains and expense, and she was yet to find the grain of truth lying lost in the gaudy debris around her, but there remained her immediate human situation, and that she could deal with, or so she believed: her mother believed in Santa Claus, or she would not have said so. The little girl did not believe in what her mother had told her, she did not want her mother to know she did not believe, yet her mother's illusions must not be disturbed. In that moment of decision her infancy was gone forever, it had vanished there before my eyes.

Very thoughtfully I took the hand of my budding little diplomat, whom we had so lovingly, unconsciously prepared for her career, which no doubt would be quite a successful one; and we walked along in the bright sweet-smelling Christmas dusk, myself for once completely silenced.

Note to A Christmas Story

This is not a fiction, but it the true story of an episode in the short life of my niece, Mary Alice, a little girl who died nearly half a century ago, at the age of only five and one-half years. The stories are those I told her, and those we sang together. The shopping for a present for her mother, my sister, in the last Christmas of this child's life is set down here as clearly as I am able to tell it, with no premonitions of disaster because we hadn't any: life was daily and forever, for us both. I was young, too. This is, of course, a lament in the form of a joyous remembrance of that last day I spent with this most lovely, much loved being.

I have a small photograph which was made on one of the interminable all-seasons cross-country jaunts by her lively, pleasure-loving young parents in the "touring car," as such conveyances were then called, and how they did tour merrily with their baby! I delight in a picture of this rumpled, happy baby, her bonnet falling off, smiling at her new shining toy of a world with serene confidence. She played the scales on the piano when she could just reach the keys, and sang them: do re me fa sol la si do: I can hear her voice yet. Her hair was smooth clear gold, just beginning to redden a little; her tilted eyes were blue as periwinkles . . .

Katherine Anne Porter 5 May, 1967

Christmas Shopping, 1947

JAMES DICKEY
(1923–1997)

James Dickey was born in Atlanta, Georgia, and his Georgia roots provide the origins of many of his works. After attending Clemson University for one year, Dickey became a fighter-bomber pilot in the Pacific during World War II. During that time he became interested in poetry. After the end of the war, he attended Vanderbilt University, where he published his first poems in the *Gadfly*. Graduating in 1948, Dickey held various jobs for the next decade and finally settled on advertising work. After the publication of his first book of poetry, *Into the Stone* (1960), Dickey received a Guggenheim Fellowship in 1961 and left the advertising world behind. He traveled in Europe for a year and wrote many of the poems for his next volume, *Helmets* (1964). Dickey won the 1966 National Book Award for Poetry for *Buckdancer's Choice* (1966), and *Life* magazine dubbed him "The Unlikeliest Poet," referring to his good-old boy persona. The publication of *Poems 1957–1967* (1967), established Dickey's reputation as a major American poet. In 1968 he became poet-in-residence at the University of South Carolina, a position he held until his death. Dickey achieved celebrity status when his first novel *Deliverance* (1970) became a best-seller and was followed in 1973 with the successful movie. For the occasion of Jimmy Carter's 1977 Presidential Inauguration, Dickey wrote his poem, "The Strength of Fields," which he recited during the televised event. Dickey claimed that, "Poetry is . . . the center of the creative wheel: everything else is actually just a spinoff from that: literary criticism, screenplays, novels, even advertising copy." "Christmas Shopping, 1947," his first published poem, appeared in the Winter 1947 issue of the Vanderbilt University *Gadfly* under the name Jim Dickey. The poem's only other appearance in print was in the Palaemon Press limited edition of *Veteran Birth* (1978).

Wingless, wayworn, aging beneath a perpetual
folded sun, despair unsounded in the eyes' drum,
these wheel in lax processional

past the cold counter and listless stall;
desire in rayon, in cellophane the dream.
Outside, the day, the frozen intercourse of streets;
glass placid, grave glitter of guilt and gift
bear single sitness to the bartered birth, recall

the lip, the sponge, the God-swung temple-lash.
But here the current of the five wounds fails,
the igneous cross no longer lights the mesh
and marrow of the hugely living. The bulging present fills
all calendars with gowns and tumbling clowns who fall
to end the sting.

I think of chestnut waters
linked back to back with autumn floating leaves,
the flow of stallions over cloud-white hills.

Jug of Silver

TRUMAN CAPOTE
(1924–1984)

Truman Capote was born Truman Streckfus Persons in New Orleans,
Louisiana. His parents divorced when he was four, and left him
in the care of elderly cousins in Monroeville, Alabama for much
of the next six years. It was during this time that Capote made two
of the most important friendships in his life, with Harper Lee and
with his cousin Miss Sook Faulk. In her Pulitzer Prize winning
novel, *To Kill a Mockingbird*, Lee modeled the character of Dill
on her childhood friend, Truman Capote. She described him as
"a pocket Merlin, whose head teemed with eccentric plans,
strange longings, and quaint fancies." Capote lovingly remembered these early years in the rural South with Sook in *A
Christmas Memory* (1956), later adapted for radio and film. By
the age of ten, he had decided to become a professional writer.
After his mother's marriage to Joseph Capote, he joined her in
New York and continued to pursue his writing, taking a job as an
office boy at *The New Yorker*, which would later publish much of
his work. Capote's nonfiction masterpiece, *In Cold Blood*, was
published serially in *The New Yorker* in 1965 and in book form in
1966. *A Tree of Night and Other Stories* (1949), included the
1948 O. Henry Memorial Award winner, "Shut a Final Door," as
well as "Jug of Silver." "Jug of Silver" was one of the first stories
which signaled an important new direction in Capote's career. It
was a move toward exploring the comic and sunlit side of existence and a move away from the haunted and nocturnal world he
depicted in earlier works. Throughout the 1950s the majority of
Capote's output, including *The Grass Harp* (1951) and *Breakfast
at Tiffany's* (1958), came from the comic side of his fictional
dichotomy.

fter school I used to work in the Valhalla drugstore. It was owned by my uncle, Mr. Ed Marshall. I call him Mr. Marshall because everybody, including his wife, called him Mr. Marshall. Nevertheless he was a nice man.

This drugstore was maybe old-fashioned, but it was large and dark and cool: during summer months there was no pleasanter place in town. At the left, as you entered, was a tobacco-magazine counter behind which, as a rule, sat Mr. Marshall: a squat, square-faced, pink-fleshed man with looping, manly, white mustaches. Beyond this counter stood the beautiful soda fountain. It was very antique and made of fine, yellowed marble, smooth to the touch but without a trace of cheap glaze. Mr. Marshall bought it at an auction in New Orleans in 1910 and was plainly proud of it. When you sat on the high, delicate stools and looked across the fountain you could see yourself reflected softly, as though by candlelight, in a row of ancient, mahogany-framed mirrors. All general merchandise was displayed in glass-doored, curio-like cabinets that were locked with brass keys. There was always in the air the smell of syrup and nutmeg and other delicacies.

The Valhalla was the gathering place of Wachata County till a certain Rufus McPherson came to town and opened a second drugstore directly across the courthouse square. This old Rufus McPherson was a villain; that is, he took away my uncle's trade. He installed fancy equipment such as electric fans and colored lights; he provided curb service and made grilled-cheese sandwiches to order. Naturally, though some remained devoted to Mr. Marshall, most folks couldn't resist Rufus McPherson.

For a while, Mr. Marshall chose to ignore him: if you were to mention McPherson's name he would sort of snort, finger his mustaches and look the other way. But you could tell he was mad. And getting madder. Then one day toward the middle of October I strolled into the Valhalla to find him sitting at the fountain playing dominoes and drinking wine with Hamurabi.

Hamurabi was an Egyptian and some kind of dentist, though he didn't do much business as the people hereabouts have unusually strong teeth, due to an element in the water. He spent a great deal of his time loafing around the Valhalla and was my uncle's chief buddy. He was a handsome figure of a man, this Hamurabi, being dark-skinned and nearly seven feet tall; the matrons of the town kept their daughters under lock and key and gave him the eye themselves. He had no foreign accent whatsoever, and it was always my opinion that he wasn't any more Egyptian than the man in the moon.

Anyway, there they were swigging red Italian wine from a gallon jug. It was a troubling sight, for Mr. Marshall was a renowned teetotaler. So naturally, I thought: Oh, golly, Rufus McPherson has finally got his goat. That was not the case, however.

"Here, son," said Mr. Marshall, "come have a glass of wine."

"Sure," said Hamurabi, "help us finish it up. It's store-bought, so we can't waste it."

Much later, when the jug was dry, Mr. Marshall picked it up and said, "Now we shall see!" And with that disappeared out into the afternoon.

"Where's he off to?" I asked.

"Ah," was all Hamurabi would say. He liked to devil me.

A half-hour passed before my uncle returned. He was stooped and grunting under the load he carried. He set the jug atop the fountain and stepped back, smiling and rubbing his hands together. "Well, what do you think?"

"Ah," purred Hamurabi.

"Gee . . . " I said.

It was the same wine jug, God knows, but there was a wonderful difference; for now it was crammed to the brim with nickels and dimes that shone dully through the thick glass.

"Pretty, eh?" said my uncle. "Had it done over at the First National. Couldn't get in anything bigger-sized than a nickel. Still, there's lotsa money in there, let me tell you."

"But what's the point, Mr. Marshall?" I said. "I mean, what's the idea?"

Mr. Marshall's smile deepened to a grin. "This here's a jug of silver, you might say. . . ."

"The pot at the end of the rainbow," interrupted Harnurabi.

". . . and the idea, as you call it, is for folks to guess how much money is in there. For instance, say you buy a quarter's worth of stuff—well, then you get to take a chance. The more you buy, the more chances you get. And I'll keep all guesses in a ledger till Christmas Eve, at which time whoever comes closest to the right amount will get the whole shebang."

Hamurabi nodded solemnly. "He's playing Santa Claus-a mighty crafty Santa Claus," he said. "I'm going home and write a book: *The Skillful Murder of Rufus McPherson*." To tell the truth, he sometimes did write stories and send them out to the magazines. They always came back.

It was surprising, really like a miracle, how Wachata County took to the jug. Why, the Valhalla hadn't done so much business since Station Master Tully, poor soul, went stark raving mad and claimed to have discovered oil back of the depot, causing the town to be overrun with wildcat prospectors. Even the pool-hall bums who never spent a cent on anything not connected with whiskey or women took to investing their spare cash in milk shakes. A few elderly ladies publicly disapproved of Mr. Marshall's enterprise as a kind of gambling, but they didn't start any trouble and some even found occasion to visit us and hazard a guess. The school kids were crazy about the whole thing, and I was very popular because they figured I knew the answer.

"I'll tell you why all this is," said Hamurabi, lighting one of the Egyptian cigarettes he bought by mail from a concern in New

York City. "It's not for the reason you may imagine; not, in other words, avidity. No. It's the mystery that's enchanting. Now you look at those nickels and dimes and what do you think: ah, so much! No, no. You think: ah, *how* much? And that's a profound question, indeed. It can mean different things to different people. Understand?"

And oh, was Rufus McPherson wild! When you're in trade, you count on Christmas to make up a large share of your yearly profit, and he was hard pressed to find a customer. So he tried to imitate the jug; but being such a stingy man he filled his with pennies. He also wrote a letter to the editor of *The Banner*, our weekly paper, in which he said that Mr. Marshall ought to be "tarred and feathered and strung up for turning innocent little children into confirmed gamblers and sending them down the path to Hell!" You can imagine what kind of laughing stock he was. Nobody had anything for McPherson but scorn. And so by the middle of November he just stood on the sidewalk outside his store and gazed bitterly at the festivities across the square.

At about this time Appleseed and sister made their first appearance.

He was a stranger in town. At least no one could recall ever having seen him before. He said he lived on a farm a mile past Indian Branches; told us his mother weighed only seventy-four pounds and that he had an older brother who would play the fiddle at anybody's wedding for fifty cents. He claimed that Appleseed was the only name he had and that he was twelve years old. But his sister, Middy, said he was eight. His hair was straight and dark yellow. He had a tight, weather-tanned little face with anxious green eyes that had a very wise and knowing look. He was small and puny and high-strung; and he wore always the same outfit: a red sweater, blue denim britches and a pair of man-sized boots that went clop-clop with every step.

It was raining that first time he came into the Valhalla; his hair was plastered round his head like a cap and his boots were caked with red mud from the country roads. Middy trailed behind as he swaggered like a cowboy up to the fountain where I was wiping some glasses.

"I hear tell you folks got a bottle fulla money you fixin' to give 'way," he said, looking me square in the eye. "Seein' as you-all are givin' it away, we'd be obliged iffen you'd give it to us. Name's Appleseed and this here's my sister, Middy."

Middy was a sad, sad-looking kid. She was a good bit taller and older-looking than her brother: a regular bean pole. She had tow-colored hair that was chopped short, and a pale pitiful little face. She wore a faded cotton dress that came way up above her bony knees. There was something wrong with her teeth, and she tried to conceal this by keeping her lips primly pursed like an old lady.

"Sorry," I said, "but you'll have to talk with Mr. Marshall."

So sure enough he did. I could hear my uncle explaining what he would have to do to win the jug. Appleseed listened attentively, nodding now and then. Presently he came back and stood in front of the jug and, touching it lightly with his hand, said, "Ain't it a pretty thing, Middy?"

Middy said, "Is they gonna give it to us?"

"Naw. What you gotta do, you gotta guess how much money's inside there. And you gotta buy two bits' worth so's even to get a chance."

"Huh, we ain't got no two bits. Where you 'spec we gonna get us two bits?"

Appleseed frowned and rubbed his chin. "That'll be the easy part, just leave it to me. The only worrisome thing is: I can't just take a chance and guess. . . I gotta *know*."

Well, a few days later they showed up again. Appleseed perched on a stool at the fountain and boldly asked for two glasses of water, one for him and one for Middy. It was on this occasion that he gave out the information about his family: ". . . then there's Papa Daddy, that's my mama's papa, who's a Cajun, an' on accounta that he don't speak English good. My brother, the one what plays the fiddle, he's been in jail three times. . . . It's on accounta him we had to pick up and leave Louisiana. He cut a fella bad in a razor fight over a woman ten years older'n him. She had yellow hair."

Middy, lingering in the background, said nervously, "You oughtn't to be tellin' our personal private fam'ly business thataway, Appleseed."

"Hush now, Middy," he said, and she hushed. "She's a good little gal," he added, turning to pat her head, "but you can't let her get away with much. You go look at the picture books, honey, and stop frettin' with your teeth. Appleseed here's got some figurin' to do."

This figuring meant staring hard at the jug, as if his eyes were trying to eat it up. With his chin cupped in his hand, he studied it for a long period, not batting his eyelids once. "A lady in Louisiana told me I could see things other folks couldn't see 'cause I was born with a caul on my head."

"It's a cinch you aren't going to see how much there is," I told him. "Why don't you just let a number pop into your head, and maybe that'll be the right one."

"Uh, uh," he said, "too darn risky. Me, I can't take no sucha chance. Now, the way I got it figured, there ain't but one sure-fire thing and that's to count every nickel and dime."

"Count!"

"Count what?" asked Hamurabi, who had just moseyed inside and was settling himself at the fountain.

"This kid says he's going to count how much is in the jug," I explained.

Hamurabi looked at Appleseed with interest. "How do you plan to do that, son?"

"Oh, by countin'," said Appleseed matter-of-factly. Hamurabi laughed. "You better have X-ray eyes, son, that's all I can say."

"Oh, no. All you gotta do is be born with a caul on your head. A lady in Louisiana told me so. She was a witch; she loved me and when my ma wouldn't give me to her she put a hex on her and now my ma don't weigh but seventy-four pounds."

"Ve-ry in-ter-esting," was Harnurabi's comment as he gave Appleseed a queer glance.

Middy sauntered up, clutching a copy of *Screen Secrets*. She pointed out a certain photo to Apple-seed and said: "Ain't she the nicest-lookin' lady? Now you see, Appleseed, you see how pretty her teeth are? Not a one outa joint."

"Well, don't you fret none," he said.

After they left Hamurabi ordered a bottle of orange Nehi and drank it slowly, while smoking a cigarette. "Do you think maybe that kid's o.k. up-stairs?" he asked presently in a puzzled voice.

Small towns are best for spending Christmas, I think. They catch the mood quicker and change and come alive under its spell. By the first week in December house doors were decorated with wreaths, and store windows were flashy with red paper bells and snowflakes of glittering isinglass. The kids hiked out into the woods and came back dragging spicy evergreen trees. Already the women were busy baking fruitcakes, unsealing jars of mincemeat and opening bottles of blackberry and scuppernong wine. In the courthouse square a huge tree was trimmed with silver tinsel and colored electric bulbs that were lighted up at sunset. Late of an afternoon you could hear the choir in the Presbyterian church practicing carols for their annual pageant. All over town the japonicas were in full bloom.

The only person who appeared not the least touched by this heartwarming atmosphere was Appleseed. He went about his declared business of counting the jug-money with great, persistent care. Every day now he came to the Valhalla and concentrated on the jug scowling and mumbling to himself. At first we were all fascinated, but after a while it got tiresome and nobody paid him any mind whatsoever. He never bought anything, apparently having never been able to raise the two bits. Sometimes he'd talk to Hamurabi, who had taken a tender interest in him and occasionally stood treat to a jawbreaker or a penny's worth of licorice.

"Do you still think he's nuts?" I asked.

"I'm not so sure," said Hamurabi. "But I'll let you know. He doesn't eat enough. I'm going to take him over to the Rainbow Cafe and buy him a plate of barbecue."

"He'd appreciate it more if you'd give him a quarter."

"No. A dish of barbecue is what he needs. Besides, it would be better if he never was to make a guess. A high-strung kid like that, so unusual, I wouldn't want to be the one responsible if he lost. Say, it would be pitiful."

I'll admit that at the time Appleseed struck me as being just funny. Mr. Marshall felt sorry for him, and the kids tried to tease him, but had to give it up when he refused to respond. There you could see him plain as day sitting at the fountain with his forehead puckered and his eyes fixed forever on that jug. Yet he was so withdrawn you sometimes had this awful creepy feeling that, well, maybe he didn't exist. And when you were pretty much convinced of this he'd wake up and say something like, "You know, I hope a 1913 buffalo nickel's in there. A fella was tellin' me he saw where a 1913 buffalo nickel's worth fifty dollars." Or, "Middy's gonna be a big lady in the picture shows. They make lotsa money, the ladies in the picture shows do, and then we ain't gonna never eat another collard green as long as we live. Only Middy says she can't be in the picture shows 'less her teeth look good."

Middy didn't always tag along with her brother. On those occasions when she didn't come, Appleseed wasn't himself; he acted shy and left soon.

Hamurabi kept his promise and stood treat to a dish of barbecue at the café. "Mr. Hamurabi's nice, all right," said Appleseed afterward, "but he's got peculiar notions: has a notion that if he lived in this place named Egypt he'd be a king or somethin'."

And Hamurabi said, "That kid has the most touching faith. It's a beautiful thing to see. But I'm beginning to despise the whole business." He gestured toward the jug. "Hope of this kind is a cruel thing to give anybody, and I'm damned sorry I was ever a party to it."

Around the Valhalla the most popular pastime was deciding what you would buy if you won the jug. Among those who participated were: Solomon Katz, Phoebe Jones, Carl Kuhnhardt, Puly Simmons, Addie Foxcroft, Marvin Finkle, Trudy Edwards and a colored man named Erskine Washington. And these were some of their answers: a trip to and a permanent wave in Birmingham, a second-hand piano, a Shetland pony, a gold bracelet, a set of *Rover Boys* books and a life insurance policy.

Once Mr. Marshall asked Appleseed what he would get. "It's a secret," was the reply, and no amount of prying could make him tell. We took it for granted that whatever it was, he wanted it real bad.

Honest winter, as a rule, doesn't settle on our part of the country till late January, and then is mild, lasting only a short time. But in the year of which I write we were blessed with a singular cold spell the week before Christmas. Some still talk of it, for it was so terrible: water pipes froze solid; many folks had to spend the days in bed snuggled under their quilts, having neglected to lay in enough kindling for the fireplace; the sky turned that strange dull gray as it does just before a storm, and the sun was pale as a waning moon. There was a sharp wind: the old dried-up leaves of last fall fell on the icy ground, and the evergreen tree in the courthouse square was twice stripped of its Christmas finery. When you breathed, your breath made smoky clouds. Down by the silk mill where the very poor people lived, the families huddled together in the dark at night and told tales to keep their minds off the cold. Out in the country the farmers covered their delicate plants with gunny sacks and prayed; some took advantage of the weather to slaughter their hogs and bring the fresh sausage to town. Mr. R. C. Judkins, our town drunk, outfitted himself in a red cheesecloth suit and played Santa Claus at the five 'n' dime. Mr. R. C. Judkins was the father of a big family, so everybody was happy to see him sober enough to earn a dollar. There were several church socials, at one of which Mr. Marshall came face to face with Rufus McPherson: bitter words were passed but not a blow was struck.

Now, as has been mentioned, Appleseed lived on a farm a mile below Indian Branches; this would be approximately three miles from town; a mighty long and lonesome walk. Still, despite the cold, he came every day to the Valhalla and stayed till closing time which, as the days had grown short, was after nightfall. Once in a while he'd catch a ride partway home with the foreman from the silk mill, but not often. He looked tired, and there were worry lines about his mouth. He was always cold and shivered a lot. I don't think he wore any warm drawers underneath his red sweater and blue britches.

It was three days before Christmas when out of the clear sky, he announced: "Well, I'm finished. I mean I know how much is in the bottle." He claimed this with such grave, solemn sureness it was hard to doubt him.

"Why, say now, son, hold on," said Hamurabi, who was present. "You can't know anything of the sort. It's wrong to think so: you're just heading to get yourself hurt."

"You don't need to preach to me, Mr. Hamurabi. I know what I'm up to. A lady in Louisiana, she told me . . ."

"Yes yes yes—but you got to forget that. If it were me, I'd go home and stay put and forget about this goddamned jug."

"My brother's gonna play the fiddle at a wedding over in Cherokee City tonight and he's gonna give me the two bits," said Appleseed stubbornly. "Tomorrow I'll take my chance."

So the next day I felt kind of excited when Appleseed and Middy arrived. Sure enough, he had his quarter: it was tied for safekeeping in the corner of a red bandanna.

The two of them wandered hand in hand among the showcases, holding a whispery consultation as to what to purchase. They decided finally on a thimble-sized bottle of gardenia cologne which Middy promptly opened and partly emptied on her hair. "It smells like . . . Oh, darlin' Mary, I ain't never smelled nothin' as sweet. Here, Appleseed, honey, let me douse some on your hair." But he wouldn't let her.

Mr. Marshall got out the ledger in which he kept his records, while Appleseed strolled over to the fountain and cupped the jug between his hands, stroking it gently. His eyes were bright and his cheeks flushed from excitement. Several persons who were in the drugstore at that moment crowded close. Middy stood in the background quietly scratching her leg and smelling the cologne. Hamurabi wasn't there.

Mr. Marshall licked the point of his pencil and smiled. "Okay, son, what do you say?"

Appleseed took a deep breath. "Seventy-seven dollars and thirty-five cents," he blurted.

In picking such an uneven sum he showed originality, for the run-of-the-mill guess was a plain round figure. Mr. Marshall repeated the amount solemnly as he copied it down.

"When'll I know if I won?"

"Christmas Eve," someone said.

"That's tomorrow, huh?"

"Why, so it is" said Mr. Marshall, not surprised. "Come at four o'clock."

During the night the thermometer dropped even lower, and toward dawn there was one of those swift, summerlike rainstorms, so that the following day was bright and frozen. The town was like a picture postcard of a Northern scene, what with icicles sparkling whitely on the trees and frost flowers coating all windowpanes. Mr. R. C. Judkins rose early and, for no clear reason, tramped the streets ringing a supper bell, stopping now and then to take a swig of whiskey from a pint which he kept in his hip pocket. As the day was windless, smoke climbed lazily from various chimneys straightway to the still, frozen sky. By midmorning the Presbyterian choir was in full swing; and the town kids (wearing horror masks, as at Hallowe'en) were chasing one another round and round the square, kicking up an awful fuss.

Hamurabi dropped by at noon to help us fix up the Valhalla. He brought along a fat sack of Satsumas, and together we ate every last one, tossing the hulls into a newly installed potbellied stove (a present from Mr. Marshall to himself) which stood in the middle of the room. Then my uncle took the jug off the fountain, polished and placed it on a prominently situated table. He was no help after that whatsoever, for he squatted in a chair and spent his time tying and retying a tacky green ribbon around the jug. So Hamurabi and I had the rest to do alone: we swept the floor and washed the mirrors and dusted the cabinets and strung streamers of red and green crepe paper from wall to wall. When we were finished it looked very fine and elegant.

But Hamurabi gazed sadly at our work, and said: "Well, I think I better be getting along now."

"Aren't you going to stay?" asked Mr. Marshall, shocked.

"No, oh, no," said Hamurabi, shaking his head slowly. "I don't want to see that kid's face. This is Christmas and I mean to have a rip-roaring time. And I couldn't, not with something like that on my conscience. Hell, I wouldn't sleep."

"Suit yourself," said Mr. Marshall. And he shrugged, but you could see he was really hurt. "Life's like that—and besides, who knows, he might win."

Hamurabi sighed gloomily. "What's his guess?"

"Seventy-seven dollars and thirty-five cents," I said.

"Now I ask you, isn't that fantastic?" said Hamurabi. He slumped in a chair next to Mr. Marshall and crossed his legs and lit a cigarette. "If you got any Baby Ruths I think I'd like one; my mouth tastes sour."

As the afternoon wore on, the three of us sat around the table feeling terribly blue. No one said hardly a word and, as the kids had deserted the square, the only sound was the clock tolling the hour in the courthouse steeple. The Valhalla was closed to business, but people kept passing by and peeking in the window. At three o'clock Mr. Marshall told me to unlock the door.

Within twenty minutes the place was jam full; everyone was wearing his Sunday best, and the air smelled sweet, for most of the little silk-mill girls had scented themselves with vanilla flavoring. They scrunched up against the walls, perched on the fountain, squeezed in wherever they could; soon the crowd had spread to the sidewalk and stretched into the road. The square was lined with team-drawn wagons and Model T Fords that had carted farmers and their families into town. There was much laughter and shouting and joking—several outraged ladies complained of the cursing and the rough, shoving ways of the younger men, but nobody left. At the side entrance a gang of colored folks had formed and were having the most fun of all. Everybody was making the best of a good thing. It's usually so quiet around here: nothing much ever happens. It's safe to say that nearly all of Wachata County was present but invalids and Rufus McPherson. I looked around for Appleseed but didn't see him anywhere.

Mr. Marshall harumphed, and clapped for attention. When things quieted down and the atmosphere was properly tense, he raised his voice like an auctioneer, and called: "Now listen, everybody, in this here envelope you see in my hand"—he held a manila envelope above his head—" well, in it's the *answer*—which nobody but God and the First National Bank knows up to now, ha, ha. And in this book"—he held up the ledger with his free hand—"I've got written down what you folks guessed. Are there any questions?" All was silence. "Fine. Now, if we could have a volunteer . . ."

Not a living soul budged an inch: it was as if an awful shyness had overcome the crowd, and even those who were ordinarily natural-born show-offs shuffled their feet, ashamed. Then a voice, Apple-seed's, hollered, "Lemme by . . . Outa the way, please, ma'am." Trotting along behind as he pushed forward were Middy and a lanky, sleepy-eyed fellow who was evidently the fiddling brother. Appleseed was dressed the same as usual, but his face was scrubbed rosy clean, his boots polished and his hair slicked back skin tight with Stacomb. "Did we get here in time?" he panted.

But Mr. Marshall said, "So you want to be our volunteer?"

Appleseed looked bewildered, then nodded vigorously.

"Does anybody have an objection to this young man?"

Still there was dead quiet. Mr. Marshall handed the envelope to Appleseed who accepted it calmly. He chewed his under lip while studying it a moment before ripping the flap.

In all that congregation there was no sound except an occasional cough and the soft tinkling of Mr. R. C. Judkins' supper bell. Hamurabi was leaning against the fountain, staring up at the ceiling; Middy was gazing blankly over her brother's shoulder, and when he started to tear open the envelope she let out a pained little gasp.

Appleseed withdrew a slip of pink paper and, holding it as though it was very fragile, muttered to himself whatever was written there. Suddenly his face paled and tears glistened in his eyes.

"Hey, speak up, boy," someone hollered.

Hamurabi stepped forward and all but snatched the slip away. He cleared his throat and commenced to read when his expression changed most comically. "Well, Mother o' God . . ." he said.

"Louder! Louder!" an angry chorus demanded.

"Buncha crooks!" yelled Mr. R. C. Judkins, who had a snootful by this time. "I smell a rat and he smells to high heaven!" Whereupon a cyclone of catcalls and whistling rent the air.

Appleseed's brother whirled round and shook his fist. "Shuddup, shuddup 'fore I bust every one a your goddamn heads together so's you got knots the size a musk melons, hear me?"

"Citizens," cried Mayor Mawes, "citizens—I say, this is Christmas . . . I say . . ."

And Mr. Marshall hopped up on a chair and clapped and stamped till a minimum of order was restored. It might as well be noted here that we later found out Rufus McPherson had paid Mr. R. C. Judkins to start the rumpus. Anyway, when the outbreak was quelled, who should be in possession of the slip but me . . . don't ask how.

Without thinking, I shouted, "Seventy-seven dollars and thirty-five cents." Naturally, due to the excitement, I didn't at first catch the meaning; it was just a number. Then Appleseed's brother let forth with his whooping yell, and so I understood. The name of the winner spread quickly, and the awed, murmuring whispers were like a rainstorm.

Oh, Appleseed himself was a sorry sight. He was crying as though he was mortally wounded, but when Hamurabi lifted him onto his shoulders so the crowd could get a gander, he dried his eyes with the cuffs of his sweater and began grinning. Mr. R. C. Judkins yelled, "Gyp! Lousy gyp!" but was drowned out by a deafening round of applause.

Middy grabbed my arm. "My teeth," she squealed. "Now I'm gonna get my teeth."

"Teeth?" said I, kind of dazed.

"The false kind," says she. "That's what we're gonna get us with the money—a lovely set of white false teeth."

But at that moment my sole interest was in how Appleseed had known. "Hey, tell me," I said desperately, "tell me, how in God's name did he know there was lust exactly seventy-seven dollars and thirty-five cents?"

Middy gave me this look. "Why, I thought he told you," she said, real serious. "He counted."

"Yes, but how—how?"

"Gee, don't you even know how to count?"

"But is that all he did?"

"Well," she said, following a thoughtful pause, "he did do a little praying, too." She started to dart off, then turned back and called, "Besides, he was born with a caul on his head."

And that's the nearest anybody ever came to solving the mystery. Thereafter, if you were to ask Appleseed "How come?" he would smile strangely and change the subject. Many years later he and his family moved to somewhere in Florida and were never heard from again.

But in our town his legend flourishes still; and, till his death a year ago last April, Mr. Marshall was invited each Christmas Day to tell the story of Appleseed to the Baptist Bible class. Hamurabi once typed up an account and mailed it around to various magazines. It was never printed. One editor wrote back and said that "If the little girl really turned out to be a movie star, then there might be something to your story." But that's not what happened, so why should you lie?

Merry Christmas, You-All or Who Forgot Savannah?

OGDEN NASH
(1902–1971)

Frederick Ogden Nash was born in Rye, New York to parents of southern stock, and spent many of his childhood years in Savannah. He was a descendent of General Francis Nash for whom Nashville, Tennessee was named. Although he entered Harvard with the class of 1924, Nash left with the class of 1925 and moved to New York, where he worked a variety of jobs. He tried a stint as a bond salesman on Wall Street, but sold only one bond to his godmother. He said he did "have the chance to see lots of good movies." In 1925, he became an advertising copywriter for the Doubleday Page publishing house, but spent his evenings writing serious poetry. Nash was his own harshest judge and decided that he had better "laugh at myself before anyone laughed at me." He focused on what he called "my field—the minor idiocies of humanity." Marrying skill and wit with mastery of rhythm and meter, Nash published numerous collections of verse, as well as a number of children's books. His first book of humorous verse was *Hard Lines* (1931). Frequently published in *The New Yorker*, Nash was known for writing good-natured human commentary in the form of pithy couplets. He was elected to the National Institute of Arts and Letters in 1950. "Merry Christmas, You-All or Who Forgot Savannah?" was published in *The Private Dining Room and Other New Verses* (1953).

The men who draws the Christmas cards, dear,
They must have igloos in their yards, dear.
They lives in Labrador or Maine, dear.
They all knows how to harness reindeer.
They puts on snowshoes and galoshes,
And breaks the ice before they washes.

The men who writes the Christmas rhymes,
They all inhabits frigid climes.
Their roofs is fluffy, I have heared,
With snow like Santa Claus's beard.
Icicles decorate their nose,
And chilblains nips their mistletoes.

I loves the artists and the bards
Who makes the pretty Christmas cards,
I loves their winter scenes and such,
But still I thinks they don't know much,
For Christmas wanders back and forth
And travels South as well as North.

I'm glad our Christmas sun arises
On buttercups and butterflies,
Our Christmas carol sounds as sweet
As if our ears was raw with sleet,
Our hearts is gay with Christmas mirth
Like on the colder parts of earth,
So cross the Mason-Dixon Line
And be my Christmas Valentine.

Merry Christmas, Marge!

ALICE CHILDRESS
(1920–1994)

Alice Childress was born in Charleston, South Carolina, and moved to New York at the age of five where she grew up in Harlem. An actress, essayist, novelist, playwright, screenwriter, and short story writer, Childress draws on her southern heritage to explore racial issues in her work. Childress always spoke out for accurate portrayals of black characters in the theatre. Her plays include *Trouble in Mind* (1956), which won an Obie Award, *The Wedding Band* (1973), and *Wine in the Wilderness* (1969), which was banned from being telecast in the state of Alabama. Her novel, *A Hero Ain't Nothin' but a Sandwich*, was named one of the outstanding books of 1973 by *The New York Times*. Childress published "Merry Christmas, Marge!" (1956) in *Like One of the Family: Conversations from a Domestic's Life*, short fiction originally written for *Freedom*, a newspaper edited by Paul Robinson in the 1950's. These pieces showcase the fictional dialogues between Mildred and her friend Marge. Childress said that Mildred is based on her Aunt Lorraine, who worked as a domestic for many years and always "refused to exchange dignity for pay."

⊤

erry Christmas, Marge! Girl, I just want to sit down and catch my breath for a minute . . . . I had a half a day off and went Christmas shopping. Them department stores is just like a madhouse. They had a record playin' real loud all over Crumbleys . . . "Peace on Earth." Well sir! I looked 'round at all them scuffling' folks and I begun to wonder. . . . What is peace?

You know Marge, I hear so much talk about peace. I see it written on walls and I hear about it on the radio, and at Christmas time you can't cut 'round the corner without hearin' it blarin' out of every store front. . . . Peace . . . Peace . . . Peace.

Marge, what is peace? . . . Well, you're partly right, it do mean not havin' any wars . . . but I been doin' some deep thinkin' since I left Crumbleys and I been askin' myself . . . How would things have to be in order for *me* to be at peace with the world? . . . Why thank you, dear. . . . I will take an eggnog. Nobody can make it like you do. . . . That's some good. I tell you.

And it begun to come to my mind. . . . If I had no cause to hate "white folks" that would be good and if I could like most of 'em . . . *that* would be peace. . . . Don't laugh, Marge, 'cause I'm talkin' some deep stuff now!

If I could stand in the street and walk in any direction that my toes was pointin' and go in one of them pretty apartment houses and say, "Give me an apartment please?" and the man would turn and say, "Why, it would be a pleasure, mam. We'll notify you 'bout the first vacancy.". . . That would be peace.

Do you hear me? If I could stride up to any employment agency without havin' the folk at the desk stutterin' and stammerin'. . . . *That*, my friend, would be peace also. If I could ride a subway or a bus and not see any signs pleadin' with folks to be "tolerant" . . . "regardless" of what I am . . . I know that would be peace 'cause then there would be no need for them signs.

If you and me could have a cool glass of lemonade or a hot cup of coffee anywhere . . . and I mean *anywhere* . . . wouldn't that be peace? If all these little children 'round here had their mamas takin' care of them instead of other folks' children . . . that would be peace, too. . . . Hold on, Marge! Go easy on that eggnog . . . it goes to my head so fast. . . .

Oh yes, if nobody wanted to kill nobody else and I could pick up a newspaper and not read 'bout my folks gettin' the short end of every stick . . . that would mean more peace.

If all mamas and daddies was sittin' back safe and secure in the knowledge that they'd have toys and goodies for their children . . .

that would bring on a little more peace. If eggs and butter would stop flirtin' 'round the dollar line, I would also consider that a peaceful sign. . . . Oh, darlin' let's don't talk 'bout the meat!

Yes girl! You are perfectly right. . . . If our menfolk would *make* over us a little more, THAT would be peaceful, too.

When all them things are fixed up the way I want 'em I'm gonna spend one peaceful Christmas . . . and do you know what I'd do? . . . Look Marge . . . I told you now, don't give me too much of that eggnog. . . . My dear, I'd catch me a plane for Alageorgia somewhere and visit all my old friends and we'd go 'round from door to door hollerin' "Christmas Gift!" Then we'd go down to Main Street and ride front, middle, and rear on the street-car and the "whitefolk" would wave and cry out, "Merry Christmas, neighbors!" . . . Oh hush now! . . . They would do this because they'd understand *peace.*

And we'd all go in the same church and afterwards we'd all go in the same movie and see Lena Horne actin' and singin' all the way through a picture. . . . I'd have to visit a school so that I could see a black teacher teachin' white kids . . . an' when I see this . . . I'll sing out . . . Peace, it's *truly* wonderful!

Then I'd go and watch the black Governor and the white Mayor unveiling a bronze statue of Frederick Douglass and John Brown shakin' hands. . . .

When I was ready to leave, I'd catch me a pullman back to New York. . . . Now that's what you'd call "sleepin' in heavenly peace." When I got home the bells and the horns would be ringin' and tootin' "Happy New Year!". . . and there wouldn't be no mothers mournin' for their soldier sons. . . . Children would be prancin' 'round and ridin' Christmas sleds through the sparklin' snow . . . and the words "lynch," "murder," and "kill" would be crossed out of every dictionary . . . and nobody would write peace on no walls . . . 'cause it would *be* peace . . . and our hearts would be free!

What? . . . No, I ain't crazy, either! All that is gonna happen . . . just as sure as God made little apples! I promise you that! . . . and do you know who's gonna be here to see it? *Me* girl . . . yes, your friend

Mildred! Let's you and me have another eggnog on that. . . . Here's to it MERRY XMAS Marge! PEACE!

Christmas To Me

HARPER LEE
(1926–   )

Harper Lee was born Nelle Harper Lee in Monroeville, Alabama, the youngest child of Amasa Coleman Lee, a relative of Robert E. Lee, and Frances Finch Lee. In 1950 Lee left the University of Alabama, six months short of a law degree, to pursue a writing career in New York City. She wrote, supporting herself as an airline reservations clerk, and in the early 1950s approached a literary agent with the manuscripts for three short stories. Her agent encouraged her to expand one of the stories into a novel. Lee's reputation as an author rests on this novel, *To Kill a Mockingbird* (1960), for which she won the Pulitzer Prize in fiction in 1961. Although Lee insists that *To Kill a Mockingbird* is not autobio graphical, she emphasizes her belief that a writer "should write about what one knows and write truthfully." Lee followed this adage when she wrote about the "sleepy little town" of Maycomb and about Atticus, Jem and Scout Finch, Boo Radley, Tom Robinson, Robert E. Lee Ewell, Mayella Violet Ewell, and Dill. The character of Dill was based on Lee's childhood friend Truman Capote. The two writers remained life-long friends, encouraging each other's work, and Lee traveled with Capote to Kansas to assist him with his research for *In Cold Blood*. Although she has only published one novel and a few short magazine pieces, Lee says "that writing is the hardest thing in the world . . . but writing is the only thing that has made me completely happy." "Christmas To Me," published in *McCall's Magazine*, December, 1961, is one of her rare appearances in print, and is Lee's reflection on a gift of friendship.

S everal years ago, I was living in New York and working for an airline, so I never got home to Alabama for Christmas—if, indeed, I got the day off. To a displaced Southerner,

Christmas in New York can be a rather melancholy occasion, not because the scene is strange to one far from home, but because it is familiar: New York shoppers evince the same singleness of purpose as slow-moving Southerners; Salvation Army bands and Christmas carols are alike the world over; at that time of year, New York streets shine wet with the same gentle farmer's rain that soaks Alabama's winter fields.

I missed Christmas away from home, I thought. What I really missed was a memory, an old memory of people long since gone, of my grandparents' house bursting with cousins, smilax, and holly. I missed the sound of hunting boots, the sudden open-door gusts of chilly air that cut through the aroma of pine needles and oyster dressing. I missed my brother's night-before-Christmas mask of rectitude and my farther's bumblebee bass humming "Joy to the World."

In New York, I usually spent the day, or what was left of it, with my closest friends in Manhattan. They were a young family in periodically well-to-do circumstances. Periodically, because the head of the household employed the precarious craft of writing for their living. He was brilliant and lively; his one defect of character was an inordinate love of puns. He possessed a trait curious not only in a writer but in a young man with dependents: there was about him a quality of fearless optimism—not of the wishing-makes-it-so variety, but that of seeing an attainable goal and daring to take risks in its pursuit. His audacity sometimes left his friends breathless—who in his circumstances would venture to buy a townhouse in Manhattan? His shrewd generalship made the undertaking successful; while most young people are content to dream of such things, he made his dream a reality for his family and satisfied his tribal longing for his own ground beneath his feet. He had come to New York from the Southwest and, in a manner characteristic of the natives thereof, had found the most beautiful girl in the East and promptly married her.

To this ethereal, utterly feminine creature were born two strapping sons, who, as they grew, discovered that their fragile mother packed a wallop that was second to nobody's. Her capacity to love was enormous, and she spent hours in her kitchen, producing dark, viscous delights for her family and her friends.

They were a handsome pair, healthy in mind and body, happy in their extremely active lives. Common interest as well as love drew me to them: an endless flow of reading materials circulated amongst us; we took pleasure in the same theater, films, music; we laughed so much in those days.

Our Christmases together were simple. We limited our gifts to pennies and wits and all-out competition. Who would come up with the most outrageous for the least? The real Christmas was for the children, an idea that I found totally compatible, for I had long ago ceased to speculate on the meaning of Christmas as anything other than a day for children. Christmas to me was only a memory of old loves and empty rooms, something I buried with the past that underwent a vague, aching resurrection once every year.

One Christmas, though, was different. I was lucky. I had the whole day off, and I spent Christmas eve with them. When morning came, I awoke to a small hand kneading my face. "Dup," was all its owner had time to say. I got downstairs just in time to see the little boys' faces as they beheld the pocket rockets and space equipment Santa Claus had left them. At first, their fingers went almost timidly over their toys. When the inspection had been completed, the two boys dragged everything into the center of the living room.

Bedlam prevailed until they discovered that there was more. As their father began distributing gifts, I grinned to myself, wondering how my exceptionally wily unearthments this year would be received. His was a print of a portrait of Sidney Smith I'd found for thirty-five cents; hers was the complete works of Margot Asquith, the result of a year's patient search. The children were in agonies of indecision over which package to open next, and as I waited, I noticed that while a small stack of presents mounted beside their mother's chair, I had received not a single one. My disappointment was growing steadily, but I tried not to show it.

They took their time. Finally she said, "We haven't forgotten you. Look on the tree."

There was an envelope on the tree, addressed to me. I opened it and read: "You have one year off from you job to write whatever you please. Merry Christmas."

"What does this mean?" I asked.

"What it says," I was told.

They assured me that it was not some sort of joke. They'd had a good year, they said. They'd saved some money and thought it was high time they did something about me.

"What do you mean, do something about me?"

To tell the truth—if I really wanted to know—they thought I had a great talent, and—

"What makes you think that?"

It was plain to anyone who knew me, they said, if anyone would stop to look. They wanted to show their faith in me the best way they knew how. Whether I ever sold a line was immaterial. They wanted to give me a full, fair chance to learn my craft, free from the harassments of a regular job. Would I accept their gift? There were no strings at all. Please accept, with their love.

It took some time to find my voice. When I did, I asked if they were out of their minds. What made them think anything would come of this? They didn't have that kind of money to throw away. A year was a long time. What if the children came down with something horrible? As objection crowded upon objection, each was overruled. "We're all young," they said. "We can cope with whatever happens. If disaster strikes, you can always find a job of some kind. Okay, consider is a loan, then, if you wish. We just want you to accept. Just permit us to believe in you. You must."

"It's a fantastic gamble," I murmured. "It's such a great risk."

My friend look around his living room, at his boys, half buried under a pile of bright Christmas wrapping paper. His eyes sparkled as they met his wife's, and they exchanged a glance of what seemed to me insufferable smugness. Then he looked at me and said softly,

"No, honey. It's not a risk. It's a sure thing."

Outside, snow was falling, an odd event for a New York Christmas. I went to the window, stunned by the day's miracle. Christmas trees blurred softly across the street, firelight made the children's shadows dance on the wall beside me. A full, fair chance for a new life. Not given me by an act of generosity, but by an act of love. Our faith in you was really all I had heard them say. I would do my best not to fail them. Snow still fell on the pavement below. Brownstone roofs gradually whitened. Lights in distant skyscrapers shone with yellow symbols of a road's lonely end, and as I stood at the window, looking at the lights and the snow, the ache of an old memory left me forever.

Going Ahead

JOAN WILLIAMS
(1928-   )

Joan Williams was born in Memphis, Tennessee, and frequently
spent summers with her mother's family in Arkabutla,
Mississippi. Williams graduated from Bard College in
Annandale-on-Hudson, New York, already a published author.
Williams won *Mademoiselle's* College Fiction Contest for her
short story, "Rain Later"(1949), during her junior year. Driven by
her desire to become a writer and inspired by her recent reading
of *The Sound and the Fury*, Williams secured an invitation from
her cousin to visit Oxford, Mississippi, for the sole purpose of
meeting William Faulkner. Back in Memphis, she initiated a
correspondence with Faulkner, and he wrote to her about the
writer's need for sacrifice, fortitude, and endurance. In 1950
Faulkner asked her to collaborate on his play *Requiem for a Nun*,
but this collaboration was unsuccessful. More successful was the
television script, *The Graduation Dress* (1960), which was sold
under both their names, although Williams remembers only a
discussion of the characters' names with Faulkner. He suggested
the title for her second short story, *The Morning and the Evening*
(1953), which was published in *Atlantic Monthly*. The story grew
into her 1961 novel of the same name, which won the John P.
Marquand Award for the most "distinguished first novel" of the
year. Williams wrote four other novels: *Old Powder Man* (1966),
The Wintering (1971), a "fictionalized" account of her love affair
with William Faulkner, *County Woman* (1982), and *Pay the
Piper* (1988). Her only collection of short stories, *Pariah* (1983),
was dedicated to William Faulkner and includes "Going Ahead,"
a story first published in the *Saturday Evening Post* (December
1964). Williams says the story is based on a childhood memory of
sitting in an old store in Arkabutla at Christmas time.

*g*n the middle of the city was a park, on Main Street, a square; there, inside a hut, Santa Claus sat, with a heater to warm him. Tad stood in line with the other children thinking what he would do; go in one door, speak to Santa, receive candy, come out on the side where the grown-ups waited. He could tell his grandfather was cold waiting, and he was cold too. Children around him wore rubber boots, though it was not raining; his grandfather said later it was because of the cold and the frost slowly melting, leaving the grass wet. He had on the everyday, heavy work boots he wore even to the barn. Usually, to Delton, he wore Sunday-school shoes, but his mother had said she did not care if they called him "country," if he looked country; he had to be warm. He had not admitted that his shoes made no difference; he always felt country arriving, bouncing along in the cab of the dusty or muddy pickup, looking down on everyone. City people in ordinary cars sped by below or, worse, crawled impatiently behind, waiting to pass. Once he had asked his grandfather, "Can we ever get a car?"

And Grandpa had said, "A pickup's always served us. Why change?"

Another time Grandpa had said, "Boy, damn if you ain't got big enough for me to carry to Delton by yourself. I been waiting a long time. In the springtime, we'll go up yonder to a ball game and the zoo. Now, I reckon I'll have to carry you to see Santa."

He had planned the trip with Grandpa ever since he could remember, but his father had said, "Poppa, you and the boy don't have any business going up there to Delton. There's too many things happening on the highway with the Negroes bothering folks in Mississippi cars."

His grandfather had said, "I'm not going to bother none of them, why are they going to bother me?"

"Because you're white," his mother had said, turning from the stove; then his father had said, "That's exactly right." But Tad had said nothing.

He had watched his father and Grandpa get ready to go to the barn to milk. His father had stomped into a boot and said, "I don't know what you want to go for anyway. I hear the Negroes have taken over downtown Delton. Everything's integrated. Things have changed, Poppa. You're going to have to realize it."

Grandpa had said, "I've never had any trouble with Negroes. I don't expect to start now. Ain't any of them going to bother an old man and a little boy on the highway."

He had known his mother would tell the story again. She had said, "Ellie Watkins was driving back and saw a pickup on her tail. She slowed to let it pass, but it wouldn't. So, she went faster, but it did. Went on down the highway that way, until finally it did go by, flying. She wanted to get home then and went faster too. Suddenly the truck came almost to a stop, in the middle of the road. No reason in the world, except to make her bump it. She skidded so, she said sparks came out of her tires. As soon as she got stopped, the truck went on. It turned off onto a side road and when she passed, she saw three Negro boys looking back at her, dying laughing."

"If you're bound and determined, Poppa, you, number one, put that pistol in the glove compartment and, two, be back here before dark, and I mean plumb before," his father had said before going out with Grandpa. He had thought they looked like giants the way they were huddled into their outdoor clothes. They had opened the door, and cold had come in and traveled the room like a whisper before the fire warmed it again after they went out. He had hugged his knees. "Mother," he had said, "can I tell Grandpa I don't believe in Santa Claus anymore?"

"Goodness, no," she had said. "You'll spoil his fun. You can pretend, can't you?"

"Sure," he had said.

This morning he had had no chores. He and Grandpa ate leftover corn bread with sorghum, and then they started. His wool gloves were worn at the ends, and his fingers had felt frozen when he came into the morning. It was twenty miles over a winding gravel road to the main highway, then fifty more over blacktop to Delton, into Tennessee. He and Grandpa had lost time looking for the pistol; then his mother had remembered it was already in the truck. She went nowhere without it, though in north Mississippi there had been no serious trouble since things had been settled at the university. But his mother had said there was a differentness: beneath their ordinary lives there was a feeling of waiting, of always wondering if something would happen.

For the first time in his life—Grandpa said for the first time in *his*—people locked their doors. If his mother went for a loaf of bread, she shut up the house. His grandfather said folks had went crazy; they ought to remember what F.D.R. had said about being afraid. His mother had said locking doors made strangers; it was as if they all hid something from each other; she was afraid to express her views anymore; you didn't know how the other fellow would react to what you thought. He thought that all grown-ups thought about was change. His father had said they had to go along with it, the best they could.

This morning nothing had happened on the highway. Cars with Negroes had passed, and no one paid any attention to him and Grandpa. Once, a car ahead of them had slowed and a farmer turned into a field, a Negro helper sitting beside him. "You see any trouble there?" Grandpa had said.

"No," he had said, and looking into Grandpa's eyes had been like looking into the cistern: he had seen himself reflected. His grandfather's eyes, his hair, his mustache were all the same silver-gray color as the flat, still water. They had gone on, looking at a sun so pale it was hardly distinguishable from the white winter sky.

Now, waiting to see Santa Claus, he stood warming his hands, squeezing them and pulling the ends of his gloves longer, the way Grandpa had taught him. Behind him a girl spoke, her breath jumping in spurts like steam, telling another child the lake at the zoo was expected to freeze; people could skate there. He tried to imagine ice-skating, wondering if the pond behind his house would freeze; he had no skates if it did. Long ago winters in Mississippi had been very cold. Grandpa had skated every year on the pond behind the house, and Tad tried now to imagine him as a little boy.

Santa Claus called him, and he stepped over the doorsill into the hut. Immediately, warming, his fingers were full of pain. He wondered how the man stood it so hot with all that stuff on his face, and why he painted his nose red. Was that what little children expected? If he had to pretend for Grandpa's sake, he would have to pretend for the man's too, he had decided. He shook hands, looking the man in the eye, as Grandpa always said to, and said, "How do, Santa Claus."

"Have you been a good boy this year?" the man said.

"Yes, sir. I guess so," he said.

"What can I bring you?"

"A twenty-two," he said. "Single-shot."

"I'll have to ask your mother and daddy about that, son. Maybe when you're older."

"I've used my dad's a year," he said. "I killed a moccasin on the back steps, and there's always something after the chickens."

"Keep on being a good boy then," the man said. "Here's a little gift. Come in, little girl. Come and see old Santa." Tad turned toward the exit and stepped out, holding the candy cane, glad he was small for his age, and hoping no one else would know he was nine.

As soon as he was out, Grandpa said, "How was old Santa?" He said, "Fine."

"He don't keep you in there long," Grandpa said.

"I reckon he's trying to hurry folks out of the cold," he said.

"I reckon so," Grandpa said, feeling better. "What'd you want?"

He said, "A twenty-two," and knew he was getting the gun from the way Grandpa gave a little bounce. "Uh-huh," Grandpa said. "What else?"

"Shells," he said.

"For shore. You need a gun, you need some shells," Grandpa said. "You asking for anything else?" Tad knew the shells were bought too. He had nothing else in mind, but suddenly he said, "Grandpa, if the pond freezes over, can I get ice skates?"

They walked on, Grandpa pulling his scarf tighter. "Well," Grandpa said. "We'll have to see."

He knew there would be nothing to see. His father would say: "Son, if we had the money, just to throw away, I'd get you the skates in a minute. But that pond might stay frozen one, two, at the most three days and never freeze again." He knew that made sense, but anything he mentioned, Grandpa would bear in mind. Once he had overheard his grandfather say, "The closest I'll ever come to heaven is watching that boy grow up." Tad had felt a sudden huge swelling in his chest. He had that feeling now, walking beside Grandpa, knowing he was worrying over how to get him something. "Grandpa," he said, "we better forget about the skates. That pond might stay froze a day or two and never freeze again."

"That's so," Grandpa said. But a tag end of thought seemed, still, to remain in his mind.

They chose first to pass the peanut man who stood outside the Planters shop wearing a plastic peanut head, carrying a cane, and passing out a spoonful of nuts to anyone who held out a hand. He and Grandpa could not understand those who did not. "Nothing like goobers," Grandpa said, tossing peanuts into his mouth.

"Nothing like goobers," he said, tasting fuzz from his wool glove with them.

Grandpa could not understand parking meters but would not spend money on a lot. Now, as they were passing their truck, Grandpa gave him the dimes and he punched in two for two hours and tried to explain. Still Grandpa said he could not understand those machines and walked away shaking his head and said, "We got to get your momma's and daddy's presents. Eat some dinner, look at toys, then get on home early like we promised. What you got in mind for your daddy?"

"I don't know," he said. "What does he need?"

Grandpa said, as always, "He could use something to hep him if he gets snake-bit."

Every year they bought his father a bottle of rye together. His father opened the present as if in surprise and said how glad he was to have his supply of snake-bite medicine replenished. Then Grandpa would say he had thought he was about to run out; even if they didn't use whiskey much, when you needed a drink, you needed it. Last Christmas, Grandpa had said, "You never know. This boy's liable to be coming in here any day now telling us he's got married. We'd have to drink to that."

"Shoot!" Tad had said, "I'm never going to get married."

"Why, what about the little redheaded girl I saw you walking along the road with?" Grandpa had said.

"Her!" he had said, and this past year had gotten off the school bus early never to have to get off with the little redheaded girl again.

Where he lived, whiskey was sold only by bootleggers — Baptists had voted the county dry — and he followed Grandpa into the liquor store with a sense of guilt. But Grandpa stepped straight up to the counter and said, "We'd like to take us a fifth of Four Roses, please, sir."

On the counter Tad put a dollar of the two he had in change. The storekeeper brought the bottle and swiftly, with one finger, separated the coins spread on the counter and counted them again. "Dollar even, son," he said. "Thank you." Grandpa gave the rest of the money, and the man said, "Merry Christmas."

Grandpa stepped back, onto the foot of a Negro customer, and turning said quickly, "I'm sorry."

"That's all right," the Negro man said. "I wasn't watching myself."

"Merry Christmas," Grandpa said."Merry Christmas," the Negro said.

"Merry Christmas, son," the storekeeper said.

He said, "Merry Christmas," and opened the door, and bells jingled.

When they were on the street, Grandpa said, "Well, we got that over with," as if he had not known what to buy.

Tad said, "Now we have to get Mother's presents; that's harder," and he followed Grandpa into another store. They went up and down aisles looking at things they knew ladies liked, and Tad spent his dollar on a small straw basket with a bottle of perfume inside.

Grandpa said, "I think you know more about ladies than I do. You hep me decide." Though the present was not for Tad, his heart beat faster at the idea of spending five dollars. His grandfather always said the money had to be spent on foolishness, meaning something his mother would not buy for herself. He and Grandpa finally decided on pearls that could be worn many ways; the saleslady showed them, hung them in one long strand down her neck, wound them once, then twice around it. "Now that's sho nuff some foolishness," Grandpa said, handing over the money. "We ready to eat dinner now?"

"Can't we see the toys first?" he said.

"Can't you wait?" Grandpa said.

"No," he said; then, in the elevator, Grandpa said, "Boy, I bet your stomach's going to be waiting when you get there."

His mother had said to remember his grandfather was an old man. "You want to rest?" he said, but Grandpa said he could go on a while longer. He led Grandpa to the counter where there were toys having to do with space and science. One by one, he picked up models of the latest planes and explained them to Grandpa, who could hardly believe how fast the real ones flew. In one corner of the store was a toy spaceship large enough to walk inside. He and Grandpa went in, and he picked up the helmet of a space suit and put it on. "Just think, Grandpa," he said, "when I'm grown, I'll probably be flying to the moon."

"Well, when you learn how to fly this thing, son, take me to the moon with you," Grandpa said.

"Grandpa, you wouldn't go," he said. "You've always said you never wanted your feet that high off the ground."

"I'd take them off for you," Grandpa said. Then he put a helmet on Grandpa's head, and they laughed at each other a long time through the transparent flaps. They decided on the dime store for lunch. It was past the usual eating time when they arrived, and no one else was there. Only one counter was open. Grandpa, sitting down, said he guessed he would have to have some fried clams. His mother had said Grandpa was not supposed to eat fried food. "But if I'm not there, he does," she had said. "I'll bet he comes home sick."

Now Tad said, "You're not supposed to eat fried things," and Grandpa said, "That's just some foolish notion on the doctor's part. What are you going to have?"

"I think I'll have the foot-long hot dog," he said.

When they were eating, Grandpa said the clams were good, even if they had come out of a box, frozen. Tad said the hot dog was good too, but when he bit into one end, mustard squirted out the other. He put his head as far back as possible and licked the bun, hearing other people sit down. When he sat up straight, he saw the other people were Negroes. Grandpa was not eating, and he said, "Are you already sick?"

"No," Grandpa said. "Come on, we've got to go."

"We haven't finished our dinner," he said.

"Come on, we've got to go," Grandpa said and stood up, taking the packages.

He followed Grandpa to the cashier and up the steps and out onto the street. Then he said, "Was it the Negroes, Grandpa?" But Grandpa would not say anything; he just kept walking.

In a little while they were in the truck again, moving higher than anyone else, and he said, "You've sat next to Negroes before, Grandpa."

"They've never set to the table with me," Grandpa said.

"They've sat in the truck, close as this," he said.

"They've never set to the table with me," Grandpa said.

"You broke open watermelons and ate them in the field." Grandpa said in a flat voice, as if something had been taken from him, "They just set right down there, with me."

It was nearly evening when they got back, after driving without speaking between frozen fields over the same road that no longer seemed the same. Lights coming on in houses and barns were like scattered pieces of the fallen pale sun. Doors were shut against the cold; no one was on the road; and it was suppertime. The only store open was where the old men stayed as long as possible to play checkers. Tad looked in, going by, and saw them. Grandpa's friends, he thought. Maybe his father had been right: Grandpa should have stayed at home. When they were at home, Tad told what had happened, and his father said, "We warned you, Poppa."

Grandpa said that he was never going to Delton again; traffic had been so heavy it gave him a nervous stomach; he was going to bed. "Would you bring me some soda?" he asked.

When his grandfather was gone, Tad said, "Grandpa ate fried clams." But when his mother took up the soda she said, "This'll help that old nervous stomach."

"Why does Grandpa eat what he knows will hurt him?" Tad said.

His father said, "He doesn't want to admit he can't do everything he did when he was young."

There were a lot of things Grandpa couldn't admit, Tad thought: what he had eaten, that he was old, that times had changed. And Tad could not tell him he no longer believed in Santa Claus.

His mother said that Tad had had a long day; he had to go to bed.

He went, but he was not sleepy. He lay awake a long time, looking out, studying patterns of the stars against the early night sky, and planning. If Grandpa couldn't change himself enough to go seventy miles to Delton, Tad thought, Grandpa couldn't change himself enough to go to the moon. He would have to go on ahead without him. He guessed he could not tell Grandpa that either.

There's a Star in the East on Christmas Morn

MARGARET WALKER
(1915–)

Margaret Abigail Walker was born in Birmingham, Alabama and raised in New Orleans, Louisiana, where her family moved when she was a young child. Walker inherited her love of literature from her parents who read to her from the English classics, the Bible, Paul Laurence Dunbar, and Langston Hughes. Her grandmother told her stories of her ancestors, including her maternal great-grandmother, who had been a slave in Georgia. Walker attended Northwestern University in Chicago, Illinois, and during her senior year in 1934 she published her first poem in *Crisis*. In 1936 she was hired as a full-time employee to work on the WPA Writer's Project in Chicago, along with Nelson Algren, Frank Yerby, and Richard Wright. Walker remembers her three-year friendship with Wright as a "rare and once-in-a-lifetime association...rather uncommon in its completely literary nature." Wright assisted Walker in her poetry revisions, and Walker provided invaluable research for Wright's classic novel *Native Son* (1940). During this time several of her poems were published in *Poetry*, and Walker enrolled in the Iowa Writers' Workshop. Her M.A. thesis was the poetry collection, *For the People* (1942), published by the Yale University Press as the winner of the Yale Younger Poet's Award. Walker was the first black woman honored in such a prestigious national literary competition. Walker then turned to work on a novel based on the family stories her grandmother told her as a child. This work became *Jubilee* (1967), the fictional account of Walker's great-grandmother's antebellum, Civil War, and Reconstruction years. "There's a Star In the East on Christmas Morn" is from *Jubilee*.

There's a star in the East
on Christmas morn.
Rise up shepherds and foller,
It'll lead to the place
where the Savior's born.
Rise up shepherds and foller.

C hristmas time on the plantation was always the happiest time
of the year. Harvest time was over. The molasses had been
made. Marster's corn was in his crib and the slaves' new corn
meal had been ground. Lye hominy and sauerkraut were packed
away in big jars and stone or clay crocks. Elderberry, blackberry,
poke weed and dandelion, black cherry and scuppernong, musca-
tine and wild plum, crab apple and persimmon, all had been
picked and made into jars of jelly, jam, preserves, and kegs of wine.
There were persimmon beer and home-made corn likker, and a fer-
mented home brew for future use. Despite Big Missy's clever vigilance with her ipecac, some of those jars of jelly and preserves and
peach brandy had inevitably gone out of the pantry window into the
waiting fingers of black hands. What the slaves could not conve-
niently steal, they begged and made for themselves. Many of the
delicacies that they loved were free for the taking in the woods.
Who did not know how to mix the dark brown sugar or black cane
molasses or sorghum with various fruits and berries to make the
good wine and brew the beer and whiskey from the corn or rye that
every clever finger learned early how to snatch and hide? When the
frost turned the leaves and the wind blew them from the trees, it was
time to go into the woods and gather nuts, hickory nuts and black
walnuts, and chinkapinks. There were always more pecans on the
place than could be eaten and the hogs rooted out the rotting ones.

If Marster had not given them a goober patch, they had patches of goober peas around their cabins anyway. Sometimes there were whole fields of these wonderful peanuts. Like the industrious squirrels around them they scrupulously gathered the wild harvest and wrapped them in rags, laying-by their knick-knacks for the long winter nights. When the autumn haze ended and the chilling winter winds descended upon them it was time to hunt the possum and to catch a coon. No feast during the Christmas holidays would be good without a possum and a coon. Of course, Vyry said, "You got to know how to cook it, or it ain't no good. You got to boil that wild taste out with red-hot pepper and strong vinegar made out of sour apple peelings and plenty salt. You got to boil it in one water and then take it out and boil it in another water, and you got to soak the blood out first over night and clean it real good so you gits all the blood out and you got to scrape all the hair left from the least bit of hide and then you got to roast it a long, slow time until you poured all that fat grease off and roast sweet potatoes soft and sugary, and if that stuff don't make you hit your mama till she holler and make you slobber all over yourself, they's something wrong with you and the almighty God didn't make you at the right time of the year. Marster, he like foxes, but what good is a fox when you can't eat him? Make sense to catch varmints stealing chickens, foxes and wolves, for that matter, and it's good to catch an old black bear, or a ferocity vicious bobcat, and nasty old varmint like a weasel when he come sneaking around, but when you hunting for meat and you wants fresh meat, kill the rabbit and the coon, kill the squirrel and the possum and I'll sho-nuff be satisfied."

If the slave did not kill his meat, he wasn't likely to eat fresh meat, although at hog-killing time they were given the tubs of chitterlings, the liver and the lights, and sometimes even the feet. After a very good harvest Marster might let them have a young shoat to barbecue, especially at Christmas time. Marse John was generous to a fault and always gave plenty of cheap rum and gallons of cheap whiskey to wash the special goodies down.

Big Missy had a taste for wild game too, but it was quail and pheasant, wild turkey and wild ducks, and occasionally the big fat bucks that came out of their own woods for wonderful roasts of venison. The Negroes were not allowed to kill these and if they made a mistake and accidentally killed birds or deer they had better not be caught eating it. Vyry had learned from Aunt Sally how to lard quail with salt fat pork and how to cook potted pheasant in cream, to roast and stuff turkey and geese and ducks, but she knew also the penalty for even tasting such morsels if Big Missy found out about it. Sometimes, however, half a turkey or goose was stolen from the springhouse, after some expert had carefully picked the lock. Most of the time, however, they did not worry about Big Missy's game as long as they could get enough of what they could put into their hands while foraging through the woods. By some uncanny and unknown reason real white flour came from somewhere for Christmas, and eggs were hoarded from a stray nest for egg bread instead of plain corn pone, but real butter cake and meat and fruit pies were seldom found in a slave cabin. Sometimes on Christmas they tasted snacks of real goodies such as these as part of their Christmas. On Christmas morning all the field hands stood outside the Big House shouting, "Christmas gift, Christmas gift, Marster." Then, and only then, did they taste fresh citrus fruit. Every slave child on the place received an orange, hard Christmas candy, and sometimes ginger cake. There were snuff and chewing tobacco for the women, whiskey and rum for the men. Sometimes there were new clothes, but generally the shoes were given out in November before Thanksgiving.

On Christmas morning there was always a warm and congenial relationship between the Big House and the slave Quarters. If it was cold, and very often it was not, the slaves huddled in rags and shawls around their heads and shoulders, and Marse John would open his front door and come out on the veranda. His guests and family and poor white kin, who were always welcomed in the house at Christmas time, came out with him and gathered round to hear his annual Christmas speech to the slaves. He thanked them for such a good crop and working so hard and faithfully, said it was good to have them all together, and good to enjoy Christmas together when they all had been so good. He talked about the meaning of Christmas—"When I was a boy on this place at Christmas time, seems only yesterday . . ." He got sentimental about his father and mother, and he told a "darkey" joke or two, and then he wished them a merry Christmas, ordered whiskey and rum for everyone, handed out their gifts of candy and oranges and snuff and tobacco, and asked them to sing a song, please, for him and his family and all their guests. Then they sang their own moving Christmas carols, "Wasn't that a mighty day when Jesus Christ was born" and "Go tell it on the Mountain that Jesus Christ is born" and the especially haunting melody that everybody loved:

> *There's a star in the East on Christmas morn,*
> *Rise up shepherds and foller,*
> *It'll lead to the place where the Savior's born,*
> *Rise up shepherds and foller.*

Then Marse John and all his white family and their friends would wipe their weeping eyes and blow their running noses and go inside to the good Christmas breakfast of fried chicken and waffles and steaming black coffee with fresh clotted cream. And the slaves, happy with the rest that came with the season, went back to their cabins, certain that for one day of the year at least they would have enough to eat. They could hardly wait for night and the banjo parties to begin. On Marse John's plantation, Christmas was always an occasion and all during the holidays there were dancing parties and dinners with lots of wonderful food and plenty of the finest liquor. Marse John and Big Missy became celebrated for their fine turkeys and English fruit cakes and puddings, duffs full of sherry and brandy, excellent sillabub and eggnog, all prepared by their well-trained servants, who cooked and served their Marster's fare with a flourish.

But for Vyry, Christmas meant as much hard work as any other time of the year. Of course, she had her chance to get whatever she wanted to eat simply by slipping and hiding grub in her apron and skirt pockets as she had watched Aunt Sally do. But this Christmas she had no appetite for Marster's delicious food, none for the gaiety of the parties in the Big House nor for the banjo singing and dancing in the Quarters, nor for anything the Christmas season meant. Randall Ware could no longer console her. She was already his and she had no freedom either. Now they would have a child in the spring and this child would not be free either. This child would belong to Marster. Desperately she pressed Randall Ware to do something about her freedom. He tried to satisfy her by having Brother Ezekiel "marriage" them in the way the slaves called it, "Jump the broom," but this was not all Vyry wanted. She wanted to be free, and more than that now, she wanted freedom for her unborn child. A number of her fellow slaves were jumping the broom that Christmas. For them it was simple, so she reasoned. They were already slaves on Marster's plantation or on his "other plantation" or from the plantations nearby, and their children were naturally doomed to be slaves. But Vyry sensed, more than Randall Ware seemed to care, that this child of a free father should be free. Randall Ware brought her gifts of food and game, but she was indifferent. He declared that he would buy her at the first opportunity, but that he must buy her through some white man and Marse John would not think of selling her to him. Laws governing slave marriage to free Negroes were very strict in Lee County. Randall Ware contended that he must bide his time. One wrong move now could mean disaster for both of them.

Finally in desperation, Vyry decided to go to Marse John and ask his permission for her to marry Randall Ware. She planned to go when Big Missy was not around to influence his decision. She would go in the midst of this Christmas season while his heart was softened and his generosity at its height, when he would be mellow with brandy and whiskey, and everything seemed to be going right on his plantation, and therefore with his world. She picked a night when the slaves were having a big party and all around one could hear the fiddlers and the banjo picker singing, "Oh, Sally come up, Oh, Sally come down, Oh, Sally come down the middle," while all the others joined in the singing and you could hear one voice louder than the others calling the rounds of the dancing.

"Evening to yall, Marster," Vyry spoke from the doorway, fumbling with her apron in her hands.

Marse John, startled, turned from his desk where he was wrestling with bills for merchandise and accounts with his drivers. He nearly let his book fall when he saw Vyry. This white-looking, thin-lipped girl always managed to make him feel ill at ease. But he spoke in such a condescending tone and his usual patronizing fashion, that she would never have known how much she disconcerted him.

"Why, good evening, Vyry. Why aren't you over at the party dancing and having a good time?"

"Don't feel like it, Marster. I ain't in no shape for dancing."

"Why, what's the trouble?" Her eyes were on the floor before her, and she did not look at him when he spoke. "Are you sick, or is something the matter?"

"Yessuh. They is something the matter. I don't know as you'd call it trouble, but in a way, I's sick and in a way I ain't, and it's shonuff trouble for me."

Marse John turned all the way around in his chair now to face Vyry. He looked her over warily, and then he said in an offhand fashion, "Well, if you don't tell me the trouble, I can't help you. What do you want me to do about it?"

She lifted her eyes then, and looked him squarely in the eye. "Marster, I wants your perrnission for me to get married."

"Oh, is that all," and he seemed relieved, "I thought it was something serious. You mean you're going to have a baby?"

"Yessub, that's what I means. I'm big all right, and I wants to get marriaged."

"Well, now that's no trouble, lots of gals are getting married around here every day, how do you say, jumping the broom?" And he laughed, but she did not crack a smile and she remained silent. Between them arose a silent question, but Vyry waited for him to speak first.

"By the way, who do you want to marry? Is it one of my boys around here or a boy from a plantation somewhere around here?"

"It ain't needer one."

"Well, if it's none of my nigra boys and none around here, who could it be? You don't mean some of these overseers or guards have been getting fresh with you, do you?"

"No sir." She looked up again and through narrowed eyelids with her face still solemn she said, "It ain't none of your boys around here, and it ain't no white man neither. This here man's black, *but he free.*" If she had shot him, he could not have been more deeply shocked. His face turned pale as death and he looked as if he had surely seen a ghost. For a full moment that seemed very long he could not trust himself to speak. Vyry looked at him and waited.

"You mean you're asking me to give you permission to marry a free-issue nigger?"

"Yessuh, I is. He ain't a slave cause he borned free."

"Do you know what that means?"

"I reckon so, Marster, I reckon I does."

"Why don't you ask me for your freedom and be done with it?" Now he spat out the words with such fury that Vyry jumped as if he had hit her.

"Marster, is you mad cause I asked you to let me marriage with my child's own daddy?"

Now, red with anger, he stood up and came close to her, leaving only a step or two between them, and his voice moderated to a low but urgent tone while his hands were raised as if in self-defense:

"You should have thought of this before you got a free-issue nigger to get a child by. Getting a child by you don't make him own you nor own the child. I own you, and I own your unborn child. When you ask me to let you marry a free-issue nigra you ask me by the law of the state of Georgia to set you, a mulatto woman, free, and that's a mighty lot to ask. There's a big difference between asking to get married and asking to be set free. Why, I never heard of such in all my life!"

She drew back from him in fear as if he had hit her, or might decide to do so. Suddenly she burst into tears and looking up at him again with the tears on her face she spoke cuttingly, "Marster, does you think it's a sin for me to want to be free?"

Her words were knifing him like a two-edged sword. He opened his mouth and his lower jaw sagged. A dull red moved again over his face and mottled the blood through his skin. Again the silence between them crackled with tension they could feel. But he was master of his situation, and he knew it. He did not intend to let that mastery get away from him. But now he tried another tactic. He deliberately moved back to his desk, and half sitting upon it, he crossed one leg and folded his arms. Then he looked steadily at her.

"So. That is what you wanted in the first place. And what do you think it would be like for you to be free? And where do you think you would go? Who would take care of you, feed you, and clothe you, and shelter you, and protect you? What do you think it would be like to be free?"

She knew he expected her to say she didn't know. She started to speak the sober thought in her mind—that her husband would do these things for her—but she knew he would consider her impudent so she thought better of it and held her peace. When she did not answer him, he went on, "Do you think you would be better off free than you are working for me? Look all around you at the poor white people who are free. You don't want to be like *them*, now do you? What is it you call them, 'po buckra'? They are free, free and white; but what have they got? Not a pot to piss in. Every blessed thing they get they're knocking on my door for it. Can't feed their pot-bellied younguns; always dying of dysentery and pellagra; eating clay cause they're always hungry; and never got a crop fit for anything; no cotton to sell, and can't get started in the spring unless I help them. Do you think you would be better off if you were like them? And being black and free! Why, my god, that's just like being a hunted animal running all the time! All over the South now they're talking about making free-issue niggers take masters and become slaves. They're not that much better off now anyway. Suppose that happened to your free-issue nigger and you fell into the hands of a cruel master? Does anybody bother you here? Aren't you free to come and go as you please?"

Again she did not answer. He was watching her as he talked, and seeing the growing bitterness in her face, her tight lips, her jaws working grimly as she occasionally bit her lips and twisted her hands, he tried still another tactic.

"I've often thought about setting you free."

She looked up now at this, and he thought he caught the faintest gleam of hope in her surprised eyes.

"But here in Georgia it's very hard to manumit a slave, you know what I mean—set you free. I don't have the right to break the law. I would have to have you taken out of this state and carried to a state like Kentucky or Maryland where the law permits a man to set his slave free if he wants to. Here in Georgia manumission is only permitted as a great reward for saving a white person's life and sometimes, in great exceptions when a slave has been very faithful, on the death of his master he may be set free. When I die you will surely be free. It's already in my will."

Now the scorn in her face was quite apparent to him. He knew she did not believe him, and he was withered before her scorn. He had no additional weapon with which to fight such scorn and he was forced to drop his eyes and hang his head. But when she still said nothing, he quickly brought this painful conference to an end.

"Now that is all, I'll have to ask you to leave. I was working on my accounts and I'm 'very busy tonight. You'll have to excuse me."

Dismissed, she turned with drooping shoulders and went out without saying another word. But now her hope was shriveled and dead within her. Her beautiful dream of freedom again seemed forever lost.

Sitting alone in her cabin door with her own bitter thoughts, she heard music. In her mind there was the bitter music of an acid little jingle she had heard the slaves often sing among themselves:

> *My old marster clared to me*
> *That when he died, he'd set me free*
> *He lived so long and got so bald*
> *He give out the notion of dying at all.*

Over and over the bitter jingle kept recurring to her, but the music she heard floating out on the balmy December air was another Christmas carol also in keeping with the season and her thoughts:

> *Oh, Mary, what you going to name your newborn baby?*
> *What you going to name that pretty little boy?*

from "Memory of a Large Christmas"

LILLIAN SMITH
(1897-1966)

Lillian Eugenia Smith was born the seventh of nine children in
Jasper, Florida. She said, "I was born on the rim of that mysterious terrain which spills over from Georgia's Okefenokee Swamp
into Florida. As a child, I walked on earth that trembled." In 1915
her father moved his family to Clayton, Georgia, where he operated a hotel and a children's camp. Smith enrolled at nearby
Piedmont College in 1915, but in 1917 studied piano at Peabody
Conservatory. She returned home the following year to teach
school. Her love of music education led her back to Peabody for
the year 1919-1920, then to Chekiang Province, China, where
she taught music for three years. In 1925, she returned to
Clayton to take over the directorship of her father's camp, and for
the next several years lived in New York, Clayton, and Macon,
Georgia. During this time in Macon, Smith began writing and
produced two novels and a novella which were later destroyed by
fire. She was the coeditor and publisher of a magazine titled suc-
cessively, *Pseudopodia, North Georgia Review,* and *South Today*
from 1936-1946. This "little" magazine reflected her stance on
desegregation and her desire to better race relations. Her novel,
Strange Fruit (1944), the story of the love between a black
woman and a white man, met with many attempts at suppres-
sion. It was banned from the mail by a U.S. Postal Clerk, banned
in Boston and Detroit, and used as a test-case in censorship in
Cambridge, Massachusetts. The novel became a bestseller, and
Smith's fame was made due to the notoriety surrounding the
book. She received the Southern Award for *Killers of the Dream*
(1949). In 1965, Smith departed from her ususal subject matter
to write *Memory of a Large Christmas,* her reflection on childhood Christmases of the early 1900's.

*C*hristmas began when pecans started falling. The early November rains loosened the nuts from their outer shells and sent them plopping like machine gun bullets on the roof of the veranda. In the night, you'd listen and you'd know *it* would soon be here.

It was *not* Thanksgiving. We skipped that day. At school, there were exercises, yes, and we dressed up like New England Pilgrims and play-acted Priscilla and Miles Standish and made like we had just landed on Plymouth Rock. But the truth is, the only Plymouth Rocks we saw in our minds were the black and white hens scratching round at the hen house. In those days, the Pilgrims and Thanksgiving did not dent the imaginations of little Southerners, some of whose parents wouldn't concede they had a thing to be thankful for, anyway. It was football that elevated the day into a festival—but that was later than these memories.

We eased over the national holiday without one tummy ache. Turkey? that was Christmas. Pumpkin pie? not for us. Sweet potato pie was Deep South dessert in the fall. We had it once or twice a week. Now and then, Mother varied it with sweet potato pone— rather nice if you don't try it often: raw sweet potato was grated, mixed with cane syrup, milk, eggs and spices and slowly baked, then served with thick unbeaten cream; plain, earthy, caloric and good. But not Christmasy.

Pecans were. Everybody in town had at least one tree. Some had a dozen. No matter. Pecans were prestige. They fitted Christmas.

And so you lay there, listening to the drip drip of rain and plop plop of nuts, feeling something good is going to happen, something good and it won't be long now. And you'd better sneak out early in the morning before your five brothers and three sisters and get you a few pecans and hide them. Strange how those nuts made squirrels out of us. Nothing was more plentiful and yet we hid piles of them all over the place. Of course, when there are nine of you and the cousins, you get in the habit of hiding things.

But on tree shaking day we were meek. We said proper verses, we bowed our heads for the Blessing, we ate quickly, did not kick each other or yap at Big Grandma.

The moment we were excused from the table we ran to the linen closet for old sheets and spread them under the trees as our father directed. We got the baskets without being told. We were gloriously good. Even the little ones listened when Papa told them not to cry if the nuts hit their heads—anyway, they didn't need to get under the tree, did they? of course, they needed to get under the tree but they said yessuh and waved him goodby as he walked down the tiled walk which led to the street which led to his office.

The one chosen to shake the tree first was usually the eldest. But now and then, an ambitious underling snatched the honor away by bringing in wood for all twelve fireplaces without being told to or washing and polishing Mother's brougham and offering to drive her out to Cousin Lizzie's; or maybe, he cleaned (with his sisters' help) all twenty-two lamp chimneys. (The town's young electric light plant was still pretty unstable; one never knew what to count on; but my father took care of that, too, by arranging a signal of two quick blinks and one delayed one, which was the communal code for *light your oil lamps quick!* Even on its placid evenings, the light plant turned "the juice" off at nine-thirty.)

Whoever won by fair or foul means the title of shaker of the tree did a pull-up to the first limb, hefted himself to the next, skittered into the branches and began to shake. Thousands of nuts fell until sheets were covered and thickening. Everybody was picking up and filling the baskets, except the little ones who ran round and round, holding their hands up to catch the raining nuts, yelping when hit, dashing to safety, rolling over the big boys' bird dogs, racing back. The inevitable moment came when the smallest girl whined "I gotta peepee I gotta—" But nobody was going to take her to what Mother called the Garden House, nobody was in that kind of sacrificial mood. When the piteous cries could no longer be ignored, one of the older boys sang out, My gosh, don't you know how? And shamed and desperate, she crept behind a bush as she had seen our retriever do. Soon she was back, holding up her damp hands to catch the falling nuts, begging the shaker to shake her some and everybody was begging for more nuts on his side of the tree, for his turn shaking, for another basket.

This was how Christmas began for us. Soon, the nuts had been stored in old pillow cases. Our neighbors used croker sacks, I don't know why we preferred old pillow cases. After a few days of what our mother called "seasoning" the picking out of the nut meats took place. This was Little Granny's job, if it was her turn to be with us. We'd gather in her room and sit close to the hearth listening to her soft easy stories of panthers in the Big Swamp when she was young, how she shot one between the eyes in 1824, and of the war with the Seminoles; and every now and then, she put a broken piece of nut in our mouths; and we loved her and her stories. But when Big Granny was there, she shooed us away, ensconced herself in a rocker in a sunny place on tile circular veranda, and as she rocked and sang *Bringing in the Sheaves*, she carefully cracked the nuts (she was good at it) and got them out whole; and she'd put three halves in the fruit jar and plop one in her mouth for the road, but finally quarts and quarts of pecan halves were ready for the fruit cake, and the date and pecan cake, and the Waldorf salad and the chicken salad and the chewy syrup candy you make from cane syrup with lots of homemade butter and lots of nuts—the kind you put on the back veranda for the cold air to harden while watchers take turns shooing the hen away and the bird dogs away and the cat.

Christmas was coming nearer. It was December. A cold frosty week was upon us and our father said it was fine for hog-killing.

This, too, was on Monday. We were all present. The hogs were brought in from the farm, two black wash pots were brought from Aunt Chloe's backyard where she lived in our backyard; and an awful thing which the fifteen-year-old—specializing in the French Revolution at the moment—called the "guillotine." The word made the blood flow in imaginations where already enough was flowing to streak the day with horror. The guillotine was a two-by-six plank nailed to two strong posts which were firmly embedded in the ground. There was a pulley-and-chain attached. It served as a rack from which to halig the hogs while they were being cleaned.

Christmas Eve came. All day, Mother and Grandma and the cook and the two oldest sister's worked in the kitchen. Fruit cakes had been made for a month, wrapped in clean white towels and stored in the dark pantry. But the lean pork had to be ground for pork salad, the twentyeight-pound turkey had to have its head chopped off, and then it must be picked and cleaned and hung high in the passageway between house and dining room, and then, of course, you had to put a turkey feather in your hair and make like you were Indians; then coconuts had to be grated for ambrosia and for the six-layered coconut cake and the eight coconut custard pies, and you helped punch out the eyes of the coconuts; then of course you needed to drink some of the coconut milk, and as you watched the grown-ups grate the nut meats into vast snowy mounds you nibbled at the pieces too small to be grated—and by that time, you felt sort of dizzy but here came the dray from the depot bringing the barrel of oysters in the shell (they were shipped from Apalachicola), and you watched them cover the barrel with ice, for you can't count on north Florida's winter staying winter. It was time, then, to lick the pan where the filling for the Lord Baltimore cake had been beaten and somebody laid down the caramel pan—but you tried to lick it and couldn't, you felt too glazy-eyed and poked out. And finally, you lay down on the back porch in the warm sun and fell asleep.

Close to noon on Christmas Day we saw them coming down the road: forty-eight men in stripes, with their guards. They came up the hill and headed for the house, a few laughing, talking, others grim and suspicious. All had come, white and Negro. We had helped Mother make two caramel cakes and twelve sweet potato pies and a wonderful backbone-and-rice dish (which Mother, born on the coast, called pilau); and there were hot rolls and Brunswick stew, and a washtub full of apples which our father had polished in front of the fire on Christmas Eve. It would be a splendid dinner, he told Mother who looked a bit wan, probably wondering what we would eat in January.

While we pulled out Mother's best china—piecing out with the famous heirloom fish plates—our father went from man to man shaking hands, and soon they were talking freely with him, and everybody was laughing at his funny—and sometimes on the rare side—stories. And then, there was a hush, and we in the kitchen heard Dad's voice lifted up: "And it came to pass in those days—"

Mother stayed with the oven. The two of us eased to the porch. Dad was standing there, reading from St. Luke. The day was warm and sunny and the forty-eight men and their guards were sitting on the grass. Two guards with guns in their hands leaned against trees. Eight of the men were lifers; six of them, in pairs, had their inside legs locked together; ten were killers (one had bashed in his grandma's head), two had robbed banks, three had stolen cars, one had burned down his neighbor's house and barn after an argument, one had raped a girl—all were listening to the old old words.

When my father closed the Bible, he gravely said he hoped their families were having a good Christmas, he hoped all was well "back home." Then lie smiled and grew hearty. "Now boys," he said, "eat plenty and have a good time. We're proud to have you today. We would have been a little lonely if you hadn't come. Now let's have a Merry Christmas."

The men laughed. It began with the Negroes, who quickly caught the wonderful absurdity, it spread to the whites and finally all were laughing and muttering Merry Christmas, half deriding, half meaning it, and my father laughed with them for he was never unaware of the absurd which hie seemed deliberately, sometimes, to whistle into his life.

They were our guests, and our father moved among them with grace and ease. He was soon asking them about their families, telling them a little about his. One young man talked earnestly in a low voice. I heard my father say, "Son, that's mighty bad. We'll see if we can't do something about it." (Later he did.)

When Mother said she was ready, our father asked "Son," who was one of the killers, to go help "my wife, won't you, with the heavy things." And the young man said he'd be mighty glad to. The one in for raping and another for robbing a bank said they'd be pleased to help, too, and they went in. My sister and I followed, not feeling as casual as we hoped we looked. But when two guards moved toward the door my father peremptorily stopped them with, "The boys will be all right." And "the boys" were. They came back in a few minutes bearing great pots and pans to a serving table we had set up on the porch. My sister and I served the plates. The murderer and his two friends passed them to the men. Afterward, the rapist and two bank robbers and the arsonist said they'd be real pleased to wash up the dishes. But we told them nobody should wash dishes on Christmas—just have a good time.

Christmas Night...
and All the Others

CELESTINE SIBLEY
(1917-   )

Celestine Sibley was born in Holly, Florida, but grew up in Alabama,
where her father operated a turpentine still just north of Mobile.
"That was real country. Oh, it was great. I had a horse, I had a
rowboat and I had a mill pond to swim in," Sibley said of her
childhood. As a young girl there was nothing Sibley wanted more
than to become a reporter for *The Atlanta Constitution*. Her
father taught her to value the *Constitution*, calling it *"The New
York Times* of the South," and her mother worked for the
Fitzgerald newspaper enterprise, so ink ran in her veins. She
worked for the local Mobile paper while attending Spring Hill
College, and in 1941 achieved her dream of working for *The
Atlanta Constitution*. Sibley began her journalistic career with
the paper covering the federal courts, and for over fifty years has
contributed a column, one of the most beloved features of the
Constitution. She won numerous awards for her news stories,
including three Associated Press awards. Sibley is the author of
several books including *Turned Funny: A Memoir* (1988), *A Place
Called Sweet Apple* (1985), and the Kate Mulcay Mystery series.
Many other writers praise Sibley for her ability to write Christmas
stories, and consider them to be among the most memorable of
her works. "Christmas Night . . . and All the Others" from her
book *Especially at Christmas* (1985) proves this to be true.

---

*I*n many ways I suspect my friend, Mrs. Arizona Bell, was a
palpable old fraud—but not where it counted. She claimed
to be in her nineties and I wouldn't have doubted it, because
on a bitter-cold night when she got herself together to sell papers

down at the corner of Broad and Walton streets, she might have been as old as anything unearthed from an Egyptian tomb. She wore a World War I army coat, which hit her shoetops (also GI issue), a streetcar motorman's gloves and a Red Grange type football helmet. (This last caused a whole generation of Atlanta children to call her "Halfback.")

The only reason I doubted that she was ninety-odd instead of a mere eighty-odd was that she showed me some newspaper clippings about her "walking feats" in the West when she was a girl, and every date and every reference to her age had been carefully punched out.

She also told me that she was a twin.

"I was named Arizona and my brother was named California," she related. "He busted his brains out riding Roman style around the hippodrome in Buffalo Bill's circus."

And in the middle of the sidewalk she would demonstrate Roman style—one foot on one horse, one on another.

She herself had progressed from the circus to play in stock, she said. She professed to know Mary Pickford and her mother well.

"Little Mary died in my arms on the stage every night for three months while we toured the West," she said proudly.

But when Mary Pickford came to town and I went to interview her, she couldn't quite place Mrs. Bell. And Mrs. Bell was nowhere to be found, although I tried to set up a reunion.

"I took sick," she told me brusquely, when I questioned her about it at her stand on the corner that night.

There was the matter of her husbands. She claimed to have been married six or seven times, but when I got interested in tracking down some of her husbands with the hope of finding some money for her, she dismissed them all as "dead—long dead."

"What happened to Ed?" I persisted.

"Married him on Tuesday, buried him on Thursday," she said briefly.

"And George?"

Mrs. Bell's taste for theatrics came to her rescue, her eyes brightened and she reared back to tell a story, the gist of which was that a terrible fate befell George.

"Found him floating in the river," she said with doleful satisfaction. "His feet was in the Mississippi, his head in the Ohio."

Husbands or no husbands, Mrs. Bell was good company and a lot of us enjoyed taking time to visit with her at the bus stop on our way home at night. She was proud of the fact that one of her credit customers was Atlanta's mayor for a quarter of a century, William B. Hartsfield. He would stop by his law office on his way home from the city hall at night and, frequently, wouldn't have a nickel to pay for his *Constitution* when he was ready to board the bus.

He not only was a good credit risk, Mrs. Bell felt, but such a good mayor that when he had opposition one term, she broke a habit of a lifetime and registered so she could vote for him. She hadn't thought it quite "nice" for a lady to vote, she confided, but there were times when the need for bold action overbalanced decorum. Once she had voted, Mrs. Bell found it such a heady experience, she joined the League of Women Voters and really got interested in politics.

One time I dressed Mrs. Bell up and took her to opening night at the Metropolitan Opera. She was so pleased that I didn't even have to be ashamed that I was impelled to do it for a story.

"Grand opera!" she exulted. "I'd *love* to go! You know I was in show business once myself."

We borrowed some finery from one of Atlanta's well-to-do matrons, who got into the spirit of the thing and sent a corsage to go with it. We did the hairdresser and the manicurist and the chiropodist and even hired a car and driver, so she could arrive in style. The only thing that detracted from Mrs. Bell's pleasure was that I had been so intent on the story, I went wearing the same wrinkled linen dress I'd been in all day.

She surveyed her glittering image in the mirror at the theater and then looked at me.

"Dear, you really should try to fix yourself up a little," she murmured.

And it scandalized her that the star of the performance, Marguerite Piazza, was several months pregnant, a state which was fairly obvious when she was onstage and which was discussed freely in the press.

"In my day," said Mrs. Bell severely, "a woman wouldn't even have gone out of the house in that condition."

In her own odd way, Mrs. Bell was as active as the Community Chest in helping people. Willie Jones, an old wino who would sell papers until he had the price of a drink and then desert his post and head for the Rose Tap Room, was scorned by most of the street sales fraternity as a no-good stumblebum. He was a wretched fellow and the nearest thing he had to a home was the drunk tank at the jail. When he was out, he slept in doorways or the gutter until the police found him and took him in again.

When Mrs. Bell found out about it, she took her fellow newsies to task.

"He's a human being!" she cried. "Ain't we all human too?"

She gave the men in the group such a tongue-lashing, some of them took Willie home with them for a meal and a bath. Mrs. Bell took him to church with her and had him drop by her immaculate little housekeeping room on Sunday afternoon for coffee, her celebrated floating island pudding and conversation. Somehow, prodded and shamed by Mrs. Bell, the newsies closed ranks around Willie, helping him sell his papers when the weather was bad and his thirst was worse, bringing him hot coffee and sandwiches and including him in their jokes and their sociability.

I'd like to say such care transformed Willie into a sober, upright citizen. All I know is that he was out of jail for a long stretch and he looked better. But then he died.

The cancer from which he had been suffering for a long time, took him one night as he slept on a cot in the room of one of his new friends.

Mrs. Bell was comforted that he "died respectable and looked after" and she took up a collection to buy him a funeral.

"We put him away nice, she told me the night after the obsequies. And then, shifting her papers about on their applebox stand, she said a thing I have never forgotten.

"Ain't it hard," she asked sadly, "for us human beings to *be* human?"

Although I knew Mrs. Bell was popular, I may have attributed it to the fact that she was a sort of minor celebrity in our town and I was her self-appointed press agent. I didn't realize how valiantly she did her small job in life, what care and creativity she brought to a very humble calling.

Christmas night is always an anti-climax. The festivities are over. Everybody is celebrated out and ready to stay home and fall into bed early. On such a night, somebody called to tell me that Mrs. Bell was ill on the street corner where she worked. I said I could call Grady Hospital right away.

"It won't do any good," the voice said. "They sent an ambulance already, but she won't go. She says she's going to sell her papers. I'm afraid it's pneumonia."

It was pneumonia, but Mrs. Bell would not give up and go to the hospital until some friends and I promised to take over her corner and stay there and sell her papers until the last bus had run at 2 A.M.

"I got to see after my customers," she insisted. "It's a bad night and they're tired and cold and they expect me to be here with their paper. My boys on the buses..."

A fit of coughing seized her and she pointed to a Thermos jug she had brought to town. It was full of hot coffee for her "boys," the bus drivers. She knew that the restaurants where they normally stopped would be closed, that the passengers would be few and the runs long and lonesome, and she had brought them coffee.

A lot of people who remember Arizona Bell think her finest hour was the Fourth of July, when on her ninety-eighth birthday (she said), she dived from the high board at Grant Park. But to me it will always be the icy winter nights, that Christmas night and all the others, when she stood on her corner—selling her papers, joking with lonely, tired people, giving her "boys" a cup of coffee—fulfilling some private, personal high standard of job performance.

I Am Dreaming of a White Christmas

The Natural History of a Vision
(Dedicated to Andrew Vincent Corry)

ROBERT PENN WARREN
(1905-1989)

Robert Penn Warren was born in Guthrie, Kentucky, and divided his
boyhood years between his family's home during the school year
and his grandfather's farm in the summers. His grandfather was a
Confederate veteran, and Warren's imagination was sparked by listening to him recount tales of the past. Warren attended Vanderbilt
University with the intention of studying electrical engineering, but
a freshman English course with John Crowe Ransom led him to
change his mind. Also inspired by his roommates, Allen Tate and
Donald Davidson, Warren joined the Fugitive group, named after
their literary magazine of the 1920s. In 1924 Tate told Davidson
that Warren "has more sheer genius than any of us; watch him: his
work from now on will have what none of us can achieve — power."
Warren was equally gifted in writing poetry and prose, and won the
Pulitzer Prize both in fiction, for *All the King's Men* (1947), and in
poetry, for *Promises* (1958). With the publication of *All the King's
Men*, Warren won critical acclaim, as well as popular success. As a
founder and editor of *The Southern Review* from 1935–1942,
Warren published early works of Eudora Welty and Katherine
Anne Porter. Warren found happiness in his personal life with his
second marriage to poet Eleanor Clark in 1952. In nearly sixty years
of writing, he published fourteen volumes of verse, eleven books
of fiction, a dozen books of nonfiction prose, and a number of
essays and textbooks. The texts, *Understanding Poetry* (1938) and
Understanding Fiction (1943), written with Cleanth Brooks, revolu-
tionized the teaching of literature in America. In 1970 Warren was
awarded the National Medal for literature from the National Book
Committee. In 1986 Robert Penn Warren was designated the first
official Poet Laureate of the United States of America. This poem,
"I'm Dreaming of a White Christmas: The Natural History of a
Vision," was collected in *Or Else: Poems 1968–1974* (1974).

[1]
>   No, not that door—
never! But,
Entering, saw. Through
Air brown as an old daguerreotype fading. Through
Air that, though dust to the tongue, yet—
Like the inward, brown-glimmering twilight of water—
Swayed. Through brown air, dust-dry, saw. Saw
It.

>   The bed.

>   Where it had
Been. Now was. Of all
Covering stripped, the mattress

Bare but for old newspapers spread.
Curled edges. Yellow. On yellow paper dust,
The dust yellow. No! Do not.

>   Do not lean to
Look at that date. Do not touch
That silken and yellow perfection of Time that
Dust is, for
There is no Time, I
Entering, see.
>   I,
Standing here, breathe the dry air.

[2]
                          See
Yonder the old Morris chair bought soon
After marriage, for him to rest after work in, the leather,
Once black, now browning, brown at the dry cracks,
streaked
With a fungoid green. Approaching,
See.

       See it.

       The big head. Propped,
Erect on the chair's leather pillow, bald skin
Tight on skull, not white now, brown
Like old leather lacquered, the big nose
Brown-lacquered, bold-jutting yet but with
Nostril-flanges gone tattered in Time. I have not
Yet looked at the eyes. Not
Yet.
       The eyes
Are not there. But,
Not there, they stare at what
Is not there.

       [3]
            Not there, but
In each of the appropriate twin apertures, which are
Deep and dark as a thumb-gouge,
Something that might be taken for
A mulberry large and black-ripe when, long back, crushed,
But now with years, dust-dried. The mulberries,
Crushed and desiccated, each out of

Its dark lurking-place, stare out at
Nothing.

His eyes
Had been blue.

[4]

Hers brown. But
Are not now. Now staring,
She sits in the accustomed rocker, but with
No motion. I cannot
Be sure what color the dress once was, but
Am sure that the fabric now falls decisively away
From the Time-sharpened angle of knees. The fabric
Over one knee, the left, has given way. And
I see what protrudes.

See it.

Above,
The dry fabric droops over breastlessness.

Over the shrouded femurs that now are the lap, the hands,
Palm-down, lie. The nail of one forefinger
Is missing.

On the ring-finger of the left hand
There are two diamond rings. On that of the right,
One. On Sundays, and some evenings
When she sat with him, the diamonds would be on the
fingers.

The rings. They shone.

Shine now.

In the brown air.

On the brown-lacquered face
There are now no
Lips to kiss with.

[5]
The eyes had been brown. But
Now are not where eyes had been. What things
Now are where eyes had been but
Now are not, stare. At the place where now
Is not what once they
Had stared at.

There is no fire on the cold hearth now,
To stare at.

[6]
     On
The ashes, gray, a piece of torn orange peel.
Foil wrappings of chocolate, silver and crimson and gold,
Yet gleaming from grayness. Torn Christmas paper,
Stamped green and red, holly and berries, not
Yet entirely consumed, but warped
And black-gnawed at edges. I feel
Nothing. A red
Ribbon, ripped long ago from some package of joy,

Winds over the gray hearth like
A fuse that failed. I feel
Nothing.

Not even
When I see the tree.

Why had I not seen the tree before?
Why, on entering, had I not seen it?
It must have been there, and for
A long time, for
The boughs are, of all green, long since denuded.
That much is clear. For the floor
Is there carpeted thick with the brown detritus of cedar.

Christmas trees in our section always were cedar.

[7]
Beneath the un-greened and brown-spiked tree,
On the dead-fall of brown frond-needles, are,
I see, three packages. Identical in size and shape.
In bright Christmas paper. Each with red bow and under
The ribbon, a sprig of holly.

But look!

The holly

Is, clearly, fresh.

I say to myself:
            The holly is fresh.

And
My breath comes short. For I am wondering
Which package is mine.
Oh, which?
I have stepped across the hearth and my hand stretches
out.

But the voice:

No presents, son, till the little ones come.

[8]
What shadow of tongue, years back unfleshed, in what
Darkness locked in a rigid jaw, can lift and flex?

The man and the woman sit rigid. What had been
Eyes stare at the cold hearth, but I
Stare at the three chairs. Why—
Tell me why—had I not observed them before? For
They are here.

The little red chair,
For the baby. The next biggest chair
For my little sister, the little red rocker. Then,
The biggest, my own, me the eldest.

The chairs are all empty.

But
I am thinking a thought that is louder than words.
Thinking:
They're empty, they're empty, but me—oh, I'm here!

And that thought is not words, but a roar like wind, or
The roar of the night-freight beating the rails of the trestle,
And you under the trestle, and the roar
Is nothing but darkness alive. Suddenly,
Silence.

    And no
Breath comes.

    [9]
            Where I was,
Am not. Now am
Where the blunt crowd thrusts, nudges, jerks, jostles,
And the eye is inimical. Then,
Of a sudden, know:

             Times Square, the season
Late summer and the hour sunset, with fumes
In throat and smog-glitter at sky-height, where
A jet, silver and ectoplasmic, spooks through
The sustaining light, which
Is yellow as acid. Sweat,
Cold in arm-pit, slides down flesh.

The flesh is mine.

What year it is, I can't, for the life of me,
Guess, but know that,
Far off, south-eastward, in Bellevue,
In a bare room with windows barred, a woman,
Supine on an iron cot, legs spread, each ankle
Shackled to the cot-frame,
Screams.

She keeps on screaming because it is sunset.

Her hair has been hacked short.

[10]
Clerks now go home, night watchmen wake up, and the
heart
Of the taxi-driver, just coming on shift,
Leaps with hope.

All is not in vain.

Old men come out from the hard-core movies.
They wish they had waited till later.

They stand on the pavement and stare up at the sky.
Their drawers are drying stiff at the crotch, and
The sky dies wide. The sky
Is far above the first hysteria of neon.

Soon they will want to go and get something to eat.

Meanwhile, down the big sluice of Broadway,
The steel logs jerk and plunge
Until caught in the rip, snarl, and eddy here before my face.

A mounted policeman sits a bay gelding. The rump
Of the animal gleams expensively The policeman
Is some sort of dago. His jowls are swart.
His eyes are bright with seeing.

He is as beautiful as a law of chemistry.

[11]
In any case,
I stand here and think of snow falling. But am
Not here. Am
Otherwhere, for already,
This early and summer not over, in West Montana —
Or is it Idaho? — in
The Nez Perce' Pass, tonight
It will be snowing.

The Nez Perce' is more than 7,000 feet, and I
Have been there. The first flakes,
Large, soft, sparse, come straight down
And with enormous deliberation, white
Out of unbreathing blackness. Snow
Does not yet cling, but the tall stalk of bear-grass
Is pale in the darkness. I have seen, long ago,
The paleness of bear-grass in darkness.

          But tell me, tell me,
Will I never know
What present there was in that package for me,
Under the Christmas tree?

[12]
All items listed above belong in the world
In which all things are continuous,
And are parts of the original dream which
I am now trying to discover the logic of. This
Is the process whereby pain of the past in its pastness
May be converted into the future tense

Of joy.

Drawing Names

BOBBIE ANN MASON
(1940–   )

Bobbie Ann Mason was born in Mayfield, Kentucky, and grew up on a farm where she remembers reading books outdoors as a child. She attended the University of Kentucky and left the South to complete her education, earning a doctoral degree from the University of Connecticut in 1972. She taught at Mansfield State College in Pennsylvania for several years before returning to Kentucky, whose people figure prominently in her fictional works. Mason says, "I basically consider myself an exile . . . and that's what gives me the distance to look back to where I'm from and to be able to write about it with some kind of perceptiveness." The publication of Mason's first book, *Shiloh and Other Stories* (1982), which contained many stories previously published in *The New Yorker* and *Atlantic*, established her literary reputation. The story collection won the Ernest Hemingway Foundation Award in 1983. Mason writes of the changes brought about in her home state by the rural invasion of fast-food restaurants, television, and shopping malls. She received a Guggenheim Fellowship and an American Academy of Arts and Letters Award in 1984. Her first novel, *In Country* (1985), was produced as a film by Warner Brothers in 1989. Her other novels include *Spence + Lila* (1988) and *Feather Crowns* (1993), which won the Southern Book Critics Circle Award for the best work of fiction for the year. Her numerous short-story awards include selection for the *Best American Short Stories* (1981) and *The O. Henry Awards* (1986, 1988). In her other volumes of stories, *Love-Life: Stories* (1989), and *Midnight Magic: Selected Stories of Bobbie Ann Mason* (1998), Mason proves again that she is a master of the modern short story form. "Drawing Names," a Christmas story, was published in *Shiloh and Other Stories*.

O n Christmas Day, Carolyn Sisson went early to her parents' house to help her mother with the dinner. Carolyn had been divorced two years before, and last Christmas, coming alone, she had felt uncomfortable. This year she had invited her lover, Kent Ballard, to join the family gathering. She had even brought him a present to put under the tree, so he wouldn't feel left out. Kent was planning to drive over from Kentucky Lake by noon. He had gone there to inspect his boat because of an ice storm earlier in the week. He felt compelled to visit his boat on the holiday, Carolyn thought, as if it were a sad old relative in a retirement home.

"We're having baked ham instead of turkey," Mom said. "Your daddy never did like ham baked, but whoever heard of fried ham on Christmas? We have that all year round and I'm burned out on it."

"I love baked ham," said Carolyn.

"Does Kent like it baked?"

"I'm sure he does." Carolyn placed her gifts under the tree. The number of packages seemed unusually small.

"It don't seem like Christmas with drawed names," said Mom.

"Your star's about to fall off." Carolyn straightened the silver ornament at the tip of the tree.

"I didn't decorate as much as I wanted to. I'm slowing down. Getting old, I guess." Mom had not combed her hair, and she was wearing a work shirt and tennis shoes.

"You always try to do too much on Christmas, Mom."

Carolyn knew the agreement to draw names had bothered her mother. But the four daughters were grown, and two had children. Sixteen people were expected today. Carolyn herself could not afford to buy fifteen presents on her salary as a clerk at J. C. Penney's, and her parents' small farm had not been profitable in years.

Carolyn's father appeared in the kitchen, and he hugged her so tightly she squealed in protest.

"That's all I can afford this year," he said, laughing. As he took a piece of candy from a dish on the counter, Carolyn teased him. "You'd better watch your calories today."

"Oh, not on Christmas!"

It made Carolyn sad to see her handsome father getting older. He was a shy man, awkward with his daughters, and Carolyn knew he had been deeply disappointed over her failed marriage, although he had never said so. Now he asked, "Who bought these 'toes'?"

He would no longer say "nigger toes," his old name for the chocolate-covered creams.

"Hattie Smoot brought those over," said Mom. "I made a pants suit for her last week," she said to Carolyn. "She's the woman that had stomach bypass?"

"When PeeWee McClain had that, it didn't work and they had to fix him back like he was," said Dad. He offered Carolyn a piece of candy, but she shook her head no.

Mom said, "I made Hattie a dress back last spring for her boy's graduation, and she couldn't even find a pattern big enough. I had to 'low a foot. But after that bypass, she's down to a size twenty."

"I think we'll all need a stomach bypass after we eat this feast you're fixing," said Carolyn.

"Where's Kent?" Dad asked abruptly.

"He went to see about his boat. He said he'd be here."

Carolyn looked at the clock. She felt uneasy about inviting Kent. Everyone would be scrutinizing him, as if he were some new character on a soap opera. Kent, who drove a truck for the Kentucky Loose-Leaf Floor, was a part-time student at Murray State. He was majoring in accounting. When Carolyn had started going with him, early in the summer, they had gone sailing on his boat, which had "Joyce" painted on it. Later, he painted over the name, insisting he didn't love Joyce anymore, but he had never said he loved Carolyn. She did not know if she loved him. Each seemed to be waiting for the other to say it first.

While Carolyn helped her mother in the kitchen, Dad went to get her grandfather, her mother's father. Pappy, who had been disabled by a stroke, was cared for by a live-in housekeeper who had gone home to her own family for the day. Carolyn diced apples and pears for fruit salad while her mother shaped sweet-potato balls with marshmallow centers and rolled them in crushed cornflakes. On TV in the living room, "Days of Our Lives" was beginning, but the Christmas tree blocked their view of the television set.

"Whose name did you draw, Mom?" Carolyn asked, as she began seeding the grapes.

"Jim's."

"You put Jim's name in the hat?"

Mom nodded. Jim Walsh was the man Carolyn's younger sister, Laura Jean, was living with in St. Louis. Laura Jean was going to an interior-decorating school, and Jim was a textiles salesman she had met in a class. "I made him a shirt," Mom said.

"I'm surprised at you."

"Well, what was I to do?"

"I'm just surprised." Carolyn ate a grape and spit out the seeds. "Emily Post says the couple should be offered the same room when they visit."

"You know we'd never stand for that. I don't think your dad's ever got over her stacking up with that guy."

"You mean shacking up."

"Same thing." Mom dropped the potato masher, and the metal rattled on the floor. "Oh, I'm in such a tizzy," she said.

As the family began to arrive, the noise of the TV played against the greetings, the slam of the storm door, the outside wind rushing in. Carolyn's older sisters, Peggy and Iris, with their husbands and children, were arriving all at once, and suddenly the house seemed small. Peggy's children Stevie and Cheryl, without even removing their jackets, became involved in a basketball game on TV. In his lap, Stevie had a Merlin electronic toy, which beeped randomly. Iris and Ray's children, Deedee and Jonathan, went outside to look for cats.

In the living room, Peggy jiggled her baby, Lisa, on her hip and said, "You need you one of these, Carolyn."

"Where can I get one?" said Carolyn rather sharply. Peggy grinned. "At the gittin' place, I reckon."

Peggy's critical tone was familiar. She was the only sister who had had a real wedding. Her husband, Cecil, had a Gulf franchise, and they owned a motor-cruiser, a pickup truck, a camper, a station wagon, and a new brick colonial home. Whenever Carolyn went to visit Peggy, she felt apologetic for not having a man who would buy her all these things, but she never seemed to be attracted to anyone steady or ambitious. She had been wondering how Kent would get along with the men of the family. Cecil and Ray were standing in a corner talking about gas mileage. Cecil, who was shorter than Peggy and was going bald, always worked on Dad's truck for free, and Ray usually agreed with Dad on politics to avoid an argument. Ray had an impressive government job in Frankfort. He had coordinated a ribbon-cutting ceremony when the toll road opened. What would Kent have to say to them? She could imagine him insisting that everyone go outside later to watch the sunset. Her father would think that was ridiculous. No one ever did that on a farm, but it was the sort of thing Kent would think of. Yet she knew that spontaneity was what she liked in him.

Deedee and Jonathan, who were ten and six, came inside then and immediately began shaking the presents under the tree. All the children were wearing new jeans and cowboy shirts, Carolyn noticed.

"Why are y'all so quiet?" she asked. "I thought kids whooped and hollered on Christmas."

"They've been up since *four*," said Iris. She took a cigarette from her purse and accepted a light from Cecil. Exhaling smoke, she said to Carolyn, "We heard Kent was coming." Before Carolyn could reply, Iris scolded the children for shaking the packages. She seemed nervous.

"He's supposed to be here by noon," said Carolyn.

"There's somebody now. I hear a car."

"It might be Dad, with Pappy."

It was Laura Jean, showing off Jim Walsh as though he were a splendid Christmas gift she had just received.

"Let me kiss everybody!" she cried, as the women rushed toward her. Laura Jean had not been home in four months.

"Merry Christmas!" Jim said in a booming, official-sounding voice, something like a TV announcer, Carolyn thought. He embraced all the women and then, with a theatrical gesture, he handed Mom a bottle of Rebel Yell bourbon and a carton of boiled custard, which he took from a shopping bag. The bourbon was in a decorative Christmas box.

Mom threw up her hands. "Oh, no, I'm afraid I'll be a alky-holic."

"Oh, that's ridiculous, Mom," said Laura Jean, taking Jim's coat. "A couple of drinks a day are good for your heart."

Jim insisted on getting coffee cups from a kitchen cabinet and mixing some boiled custard and bourbon. When he handed a cup to Mom, she puckered up her face.

"Law, don't let the preacher in," she said, taking a sip. "Boy, that sends my blood pressure up.

Carolyn waved away the drink that Jim offered her. "I don't start this early in the day," she said, feeling confused.

Jim was a large, dark-haired man with a neat little beard, like a bird's nest cupped on his chin. He had a northern accent. When he hugged her, Carolyn caught a whiff of cologne, something sweet, like chocolate syrup. Last summer, when Laura Jean had brought him home for the first time, she had made a point of kissing and hugging him in front of everyone. Dad had virtually ignored him. Now Carolyn saw that Jim was telling Cecil that he always bought Gulf gas. Red-faced, Ray accepted a cup of boiled custard.

Carolyn fled to the kitchen and began grating cheese for potatoes au gratin. She dreaded Kent's arrival.

When Dad arrived with Pappy, Cecil and Jim helped set up the wheelchair in a corner. Afterward, Dad and Jim shook hands, and Dad refused Jim's offer of bourbon. From the kitchen, Carolyn could see Dad hugging Laura Jean, not letting go. She went into the living room to greet her grandfather.

"They roll me in this buggy too fast," he said when she kissed his forehead.

Carolyn hoped he wouldn't notice the bottle of bourbon, but she knew he never missed anything. He was so deaf people had given up talking to him. Now the children tiptoed around him, looking at him with awe. Somehow, Carolyn expected the children to notice that she was alone, like Pappy.

At ten minutes of one, the telephone rang. Peggy answered and handed the receiver to Carolyn. "It's Kent," she said.

Kent had not left the lake yet. "I just got here an hour ago," he told Carolyn. "I had to take my sister over to my mother's."

"Is the boat OK?"

"Yeah. Just a little scraped paint. I'll be ready to go in a little while." He hesitated, as though waiting for assurance that the invitation was real.

"This whole gang's ready to eat," Carolyn said. "Can't you hurry?" She should have remembered the way he tended to get sidetracked. Once it took them three hours to get to Paducah, because he kept stopping at antique shops.

After she hung up the telephone, her mother asked, "Should I put the rolls in to brown yet?"

"Wait just a little. He's just now leaving the lake."

"When's this Kent feller coming?" asked Dad impatiently, as he peered into the kitchen. "It's time to eat."

"He's on his way," said Carolyn.

"Did you tell him we don't wait for stragglers?"

"No."

"When the plate rattles, we eat."

"I know."

"Did you tell him that?"

"No, I didn't!" cried Carolyn, irritated.

When they were alone in the kitchen, Carolyn's mother said to her, "Your dad's not hisself today. He's fit to be tied about Laura Jean bringing that guy down here again. And him bringing that whiskey."

"That was uncalled for," Carolyn agreed. She had noticed that Mom had set her cup of eggnog in the refrigerator.

"Besides, he's not too happy about that Kent Ballard you're running around with."

"What's it to him?"

"You know how he always was. He don't think anybody's good enough for one of his little girls, and he's afraid you'll get mistreated again. He don't think Kent's very dependable."

"I guess Kent's proving Dad's point."

Carolyn's sister Iris had dark brown eyes, unique in the family. When Carolyn was small, she tried to say "Iris's eyes" once and called them "Irish eyes," confusing them with a song their mother sometimes sang, "When Irish Eyes Are Smiling." Thereafter, they always teased Iris about her smiling Irish eyes. Today Iris was not smiling. Carolyn found her in a bedroom smoking, holding an ashtray in her hand.

"I drew your name," Carolyn told her. "I got you something I wanted myself."

"Well, if I don't want it, I guess I'll have to give it to you."

"What's wrong with you today?"

"Ray and me's getting a separation," said Iris.

"Really?" Carolyn was startled by the note of glee in her response. Actually, she told herself later, it was because she was glad her sister, whom she saw infrequently, had confided in her.

"The thing of it is, I had to beg him to come today, for Mom and Dad's sake. It'll kill them. Don't let on, will you?"

"I won't. What are you going to do?"

"I don't know. He's already moved out." "Are you going to stay in Frankfort?" "I don't know. I have to work things out."

Mom stuck her head in the door. "Well, is Kent coming or not?"

"He *said* he'd be here," said Carolyn.

"Your dad's about to have a duck with a rubber tail. He can't stand to wait on a meal."

"Well, let's go ahead then. Kent can eat when he gets here." When Mom left, Iris said, "Aren't you and Kent getting along?"

"I don't know. He said he'd come today, but I have a feeling he doesn't really want to."

"To hell with men." Iris laughed and stubbed out her cigarette. "Just look at us, didn't we turn out awful? First your divorce. Now me. And Laura Jean bringing that guy down. Daddy can't stand him. Did you see the look he gave him?"

"Laura Jean's got a lot more nerve than I've got," said Carolyn, nodding. "I could wring Kent's neck for being late. Well, none of us can do anything right-except Peggy."

"Daddy's precious little angel," said Iris mockingly. "Come on, we'd better get in there and help."

While Mom went to change her blouse and put on lipstick, the sisters brought the food into the dining room. Two tables had been put together. Peggy cut the ham with an electric knife, and Carolyn filled the iced-tea glasses.

"Pappy gets buttermilk and Stevie gets Coke," Peggy directed her.

"I know," said Carolyn, almost snapping.

As the family sat down, Carolyn realized that no one ever asked Pappy to "turn thanks" anymore at holiday dinners. He was sitting there expectantly, as if waiting to be asked. Mom cut up his ham into small bits. Carolyn waited for a car to drive up, the phone to ring. The TV was still on.

"Y'all dig in," said Mom. "Jim? Make sure you try some of these dressed eggs like I fix."

"I thought your new boyfriend was coming," said Cecil to Carolyn. "So did I!" said Laura Jean. "That's what you wrote me. Everyone looked at Carolyn as she explained. She looked away.

"You're looking at that pitiful tree," Mom said to her. "I just know it don't show up good from the road."

"No, it looks fine." No one had really noticed the tree. Carolyn seemed to be seeing it for the first time in years-broken red-plastic reindeer, Styrofoam snowmen with crumbling top hats, silver walnuts, which she remembered painting when she was about twelve.

Dad began telling a joke about some monks who had taken a vow of silence. At each Christmas dinner, he said, one monk was allowed to speak.

"Looks like your vocal cords would rust out," said Cheryl. "Shut up, Cheryl. Granddaddy's trying to tell something," said Cecil.

"So the first year it was the first monk's turn to talk, and you know what he said? He said, 'These taters is lumpy.'

When several people laughed, Stevie asked, "Is that the joke?"

Carolyn was baffled. Her father had never told a joke at the table in his life. He sat at the head of the table, looking out past the family at the cornfield through the picture window.

"Pay attention, now," he said. "The second year Christmas rolled around again and it was the second monk's turn to say something. He said, 'You know, I think you're right. The taters is lumpy.'

Laura Jean and Jim laughed loudly.

"Reach me some light bread," said Pappy. Mom passed the dish around the table to him.

"And so the third year," Dad continued, "the third monk got to say something. What he said-" Dad was suddenly overcome with mirth-"what he said was, 'If y'all don't shut up arguing about them taters, I'm going to leave this place!'

After the laughter died, Mom said, "Can you imagine anybody not atalking all year long?"

"That's the way monks are, Mom," said Laura Jean. "Monks

are economical with everything. They're not wasteful, not even with words."

"The Trappist monks are really an outstanding group," said Jim. "And they make excellent bread. No preservatives."

Cecil and Peggy stared at Jim.

"You're not eating, Dad," said Carolyn. She was sitting between him and the place set for Kent. The effort at telling the joke seemed to have taken her father's appetite.

"He ruined his dinner on nigger toes," said Mom.

"Dottie Barlow got a Barbie doll for Christmas and it's black," Cheryl said.

"Dottie Barlow ain't black, is she?" asked Cecil.

"That's funny," said Peggy. "Why would they give her a black Barbie doll?"

"She just wanted it."

Abruptly, Dad left the table, pushing back his plate. He sat down in the recliner chair in front of the TV. The Blue-Gray game was beginning, and Cecil and Ray were hurriedly finishing in order to join him. Carolyn took out second helpings of ham and Jell-O salad, feeling as though she was eating for Kent in his absence. Jim was taking seconds of everything, complimenting Mom. Mom apologized for not having fancy napkins. Then Laura Jean described a photography course she had taken. She had been photographing close-ups of car parts-fenders, headlights, mud flaps.

"That sounds goofy," said one of the children, Deedee.

Suddenly Pappy spoke. "Use to, the menfolks would eat first, and the children separate. The womenfolks would eat last, in the kitchen."

"You know what I could do with you all, don't you?" said Mom, shaking her fist at him. "I could set up a plank out in the field for y'all to eat on." She laughed.

"Times are different now, Pappy," said Iris loudly. "We're just as good as the men."

"She gets that from television," said Ray, with an apologetic laugh.

Carolyn noticed Ray's glance at Iris. Just then Iris matter-of-factly plucked an eyelash from Ray's cheek. It was as though she had momentarily forgotten about the separation.

Later, after the gifts were opened, Jim helped clear the tables. Kent still had not come. The baby slept, and Laura Jean, Jim, Peggy, and Mom played a *Star Trek* board game at the dining room table, while Carolyn and Iris played "Battlestar Galactica" with Cheryl and Deedee. The other men were quietly engrossed in a football game, a blur of sounds. No one had mentioned Kent's absence, but after the children had distributed the gifts, Carolyn refused to tell them what was in the lone package left under the tree. It was the most extravagantly wrapped of all the presents, with an immense ribbon, not a stick-on bow. An icicle had dropped on it, and it reminded Carolyn of an abandoned float from a parade.

At a quarter to three, Kent telephoned. He was still at the lake. "The gas stations are all closed," he said. "I couldn't get any gas."

"We already ate and opened the presents," said Carolyn.

"Here I am, stranded. Not a thing I can do about it."

Kent's voice was shaky and muffled, and Carolyn suspected he had been drinking. She did not know what to say, in front of the family. She chattered idly, while she played with a ribbon from a package. The baby was awake, turning dials and knobs on a Busy Box. On TV, the Blues picked up six yards on an end sweep. Carolyn fixed her eyes on the tilted star at the top of the tree. Kent was saying something about Santa Claus.

"They wanted me to play Santy at Mama's house for the littl'uns. I said-you know what I said? 'Bah, humbug!' Did I ever tell you what I've got against Christmas?"

"Maybe not." Carolyn's back stiffened against the wall.

"When I was little bitty, Santa Claus came to town. I was about five. I was all fired up to go see Santy, and Mama took me, but we

were late, and he was about to leave. I had to run across the courthouse square to get to him. He was giving away suckers, so I ran as
hard as I could. He was climbing up on the fire engine-are you listening?"

"Unh-huh." Carolyn was watching her mother, who was fold-
ing Christmas paper to save for next year.

Kent said, "I reached up and pulled at his old red pants leg, and
he looked down at me, and you know what he said?"

"No, what?"

"He said, 'Piss off, kid.'"

"Really?"

"Would I lie to you?"

"I don't know."

"Do you want to hear the rest of my hard-luck story?"

"Not now."

"Oh, I forgot this was long-distance. I'll call you tomorrow.
Maybe I'll go paint the boat. That's what I'll do! I'll go paint it right
this minute."

After Carolyn hung up the telephone, her mother said, "I think
my Oriental casserole was a failure. I used the wrong kind of mushroom soup. It called for cream of mushroom and I used golden
mushroom."

"Won't you *ever* learn, Mom?" cried Carolyn. "You always cook
too much. You make *such* a big deal—"

Mom said, "What happened with Kent this time?"

"He couldn't get gas. He forgot the gas stations were closed."

"Jim and Laura Jean didn't have any trouble getting gas," said
Peggy, looking up from the game.

"We tanked up yesterday," said Laura Jean.

"Of course you did," said Carolyn distractedly. "You always
think ahead."

"It's your time," Cheryl said, handing Carolyn the "Battlestar
Galactica" toy. "I did lousy."

"Not as lousy as I did," said Iris.

Carolyn tried to concentrate on shooting enemy missiles raining through space. Her sisters seemed far away, like the spaceships. She was aware of the men watching football, their hands in action as they followed an exciting play. Even though Pappy had fallen asleep, with his blanket in his lap he looked like a king on a throne. Carolyn thought of the quiet accommodation her father had made to his father-in-law, just as Cecil and Ray had done with Dad, and her ex-husband had tried to do once. But Cecil had bought his way in, and now Ray was getting out. Kent had stayed away. Jim, the newcomer, was with the women, playing *Star Trek* as if his life depended upon it. Carolyn was glad now that Kent had not come. The story he had told made her angry, and his pity for his childhood make her think of something Pappy had often said—"Christmas is for children." Earlier, she had listened in amazement while Cheryl listed on her fingers the gifts she had received that morning: a watch, a stereo, a nightgown, hot curls, perfume, candles, a sweater, a calculator, a jewelry box, a ring. Now Carolyn saw Kent's boat as his toy, more important to him than the family obligations of the holiday.

Mom was saying, "I wanted to make a Christmas tablecloth out of red checks with green fringe. You wouldn't think knit would do for a tablecloth, but Hattie Smoot has the prettiest one."

"You can do incredible things with knit," said Jim with sudden enthusiasm. The shirt Mom had made him was bonded knit.

"Who's Hattie Smoot?" asked Laura Jean. She was caressing the back of Jim's neck, as though soothing his nerves.

Carolyn laughed when her mother began telling Jim and Laura Jean about Hattie Smoot's operation. Jim listened attentively, leaning forward with his elbows on the table, and asked eager questions, his eyes as alert as Pappy's.

"Is she telling a joke?" Cheryl asked Carolyn.

"No. I'm not laughing at you, Mom," Carolyn said, touching her mother's hand. She felt relieved that the anticipation of Christmas had ended. Still laughing, she said, "Pour me some of that Rebel Yell, Jim. It's time."

"I'm with you," Jim said, jumping up.

In the kitchen, Carolyn located a clean spoon while Jim washed some cups. Carolyn couldn't find the cup Mom had left in the refrigerator. As she took out the carton of boiled custard, Jim said, "It must be a very difficult day for you."

Carolyn was startled. His tone was unexpectedly kind, genuine. She was struck suddenly by what he must know about her, because of his intimacy with her sister. She knew nothing about him. When he smiled, she saw a gold cap on a molar, shining like a Christmas ornament. She managed to say, "It can't be any picnic for you, either. Kent didn't want to put up with us."

"Too bad he couldn't get gas."

"I don't think he wanted to get gas.

"Then you're better off without him." When Jim looked at her, Carolyn felt that he must be examining her resemblance to Laura Jean. He said, "I think your family's great."

Carolyn laughed nervously. "We're hard on you. God, you're brave to come down here like this."

"Well, Laura Jean's worth it."

They took the boiled custard and cups into the dining room. As Carolyn sat down, her nephew Jonathan begged her to tell what was in the gift left under the tree.

"I can't tell," she said.

"Why not?"

"I'm saving it till next year, in case I draw some man's name.

"I hope it's mine," said Jonathan.

Jim stirred bourbon into three cups of boiled custard, and gave one to Carolyn and one to Laura Jean. The others had declined. Then he leaned back in his chair—more relaxed now—and squeezed Laura Jean's hand. Carolyn wondered what they said to each other when they were alone, in St. Louis. She knew with certainty that they would not be economical with words, like the monks in the story. She longed to be with them, to hear what they would say. She noticed her mother picking at a hangnail, quietly ignoring the bourbon. Looking at the bottle's gift box, which showed an old-fashioned scene, children on sleds in the snow, Carolyn thought of Kent's boat again. She felt she was in that snowy scene now with Laura Jean and Jim, sailing in Kent's boat into the winter breeze, into falling snow. She thought of how silent it was out on the lake, as though the whiteness of the snow were the absence of sound.

"Cheers!" she said to Jim, lifting her cup.

from "One Writer's Beginnings"

EUDORA WELTY
(1909–   )

Eudora Welty was born in Jackson, Mississippi, the first child and only
daughter of Christian and Chestina Andrews Welty. Reading and
writing played a major part in her childhood, as well as library trips
and books and stories read aloud to her by her parents. She completed her undergraduate degree at the University of Wisconsin
and attended the Columbia School of Business from 1930–1931.
She embraced the theater and art gallery worlds of New York City,
but faced with the job market of the Great Depression and the
news of her father's diagnosis with leukemia, Welty returned home
to Jackson in 1931. The early death of her father was a great personal loss to Welty, but she soon put his typewriter to use and
began writing short stories. She also found work writing for the
local radio station and covering society news for area newspapers.
Then she took a job which allowed her to hone her skills of obser-
vation, that of "junior publicity agent" for the Works Progress
Administration. Welty traveled all over Mississippi, to county and
state fairs, canning factories, market days, and Fourth of July cele-
brations, and documented the people of her home state with photographs later collected in *One Time, One Place: Mississippi in the
Depression* (1971). In 1936 her first important short story, "Death
of a Traveling Salesman," was published in *Manuscript* and later
included in her first collection of short stories, *Curtain of Green*
(1941). Welty is recognized as a master of the short story form, but
has also enjoyed success with her novels, including *The Optimists's
Daughter* (1972), winner of the Pulitzer Prize in fiction. Her many
other honors include numerous O. Henry Prize Awards, the Gold
Medal for Fiction in 1972, given by the National Institute of Arts
and Letters, and in 1996 the Legion d'Honneur Award, one of the
most prestigious awards in the world. In *One Writer's Beginnings*
(1984), she tells in "a continuous thread of revelation" how her
family and her sense of place contributed to the shaping, not only
of her personality, but of her writing. In this passage from the
book's chapter "Listening," Welty shares a recollection of
Christmas with the reader.

⊤⊤

*F*rom our earliest Christmas times, Santa Claus brought us toys that instruct boys and girls (separately) how to build things—stone blocks cut to the castle-building style, Tinker Toys, and Erector sets. Daddy made for us himself elaborate kites that needed to be taken miles out of town to a pasture long enough (and my father was not afraid of horses and cows watching) for him to run with and get up on a long cord to which my mother held the spindle, and then we children were given it to hold, tugging like something alive at our hands. They were beautiful, sound, shapely box kites, smelling delicately of office glue for their entire short lives. And of course, as soon as the boys attained anywhere near the right age, there was an electric train, the engine with its pea-sized working headlight, its line of cars, tracks equipped with switches, semaphores, its station, its bridges, and its tunnel, which blocked off all other traffic in the upstairs hall. Even from downstairs, and through the cries of excited children, the elegant rush and click of the train could be heard through the ceiling, running around and around its figure eight.

All of this, but especially the train, represents my father's fondest beliefs—in progress, in the future. With these gifts, he was preparing his children.

from "A Different Kind of Christmas"

ALEX HALEY
(1921–1992)

Alex Murray Palmer Haley was born in Ithaca, New York, while both his parents were attending graduate school. When he was six weeks old, the Haleys moved to his mother's home in Henning, Tennessee. His father returned to New York to finish his graduate studies, and left Alex in the care of his mother and the women of the Haley family. Haley's childhood was spent listening to these women talk of the past and of the hardships that had been endured by their African ancestors. After he graduated from high school at the age of fifteen, Haley attended several colleges before enlisting in the U.S. Coast Guard at eighteen. He wrote to alleviate the boredom he experienced aboard ship, and penned adventure stories and love letters for his shipmates. Haley became the first chief journalist of the Coast Guard in 1949 and retired in 1959, after serving twenty years. Determined to make it as a writer, Haley moved to Greenwich Village, where he lived a hand-to-mouth existence for several years. His break came in 1962 when *Playboy* assigned him to interview jazz musician Miles Davis. *Playboy* then established a new series, the "Playboy Interview." Haley's interview with Malcolm X was so successful, he was commissioned to write *The Autobiography of Malcolm X* (1965), which became a best-seller. After completing *Malcolm X*, Haley began research on his own genealogy and twelve years later his efforts resulted in his renowned book *Roots: The Saga of an American Family* (1976), for which he won the Pulitzer Prize in nonfiction. *Roots* became a bestseller after the airing of a television mini-series based on the saga. Vernon Jordan called it "the single most spectacular educational experience in race relations in America." The following is an excerpt from Haley's *A Different Kind of Christmas* (1988), which is dedicated "to the memory of all those whose courage, daring, and self-sacrifice made the Underground Railroad possible."

*D*uring the Christmas Eve lunchtime, Melissa Anne Aaron
hotly challenged her father's decision not to attend the
church nativity pageant in order to go on volunteer duty
with the patrollers. Her arguing escalated until finally she shouted,
"Father, you've no right to call yourself a Christian!"

Mr. Aaron glared at her angrily. "Don't you go too far!"

Mrs. Aaron tended to support their daughter. "Dear, she's
right—once a year isn't too much to go to church."

Outnumbered and harassed, Mr. Aaron blew up.

"I'd hoped you wouldn't push me too far!" he barked at his
daughter. "But since you do, I'm your father, and I'm outright for-
bidding your marrying this parson! I'm as much as any man for reli-
gion, but I won't permit my only daughter's hardheadedness to keep
her from someone able to give her a decent life."

"All right, but if I can't marry who I want to, I'll pledge my soul
I'll sure never marry who *you* want!"

"One day you'll wish you had!"

"If I can't marry him"—Melissa Anne was furious—"at least I
can help him tonight."

In her fury, she bangled on the dining-table bell. The maid
appeared, nervous, knowing the hotheaded Melissa Anne. "Go
bring that black harmonica player up onto the porch!" Melissa
Anne commanded.

When Harpin' John arrived, Melissa Anne snapped, "Go hitch
up the buggy. I want you to drive me to the church!"

As Harpin' John stood aghast, she added, "I want you to stay for
the afternoon rehearsal and pull the curtain between the acts as we
rehearse."

Harpin' John protested. "But ma'am, I'm the only one know
when to take off my barbecue when it just right done an' ready. I
mean, ma'am, I just got to be there!" He needed that afternoon des-

perately, not only to set up the barbecue, but to oversee final details of the escape, to reduce the chances of anything going wrong.

Melissa Anne had been spoiling for a tantrum.

She shrieked, "You heard me! You're a hired darky! You do as I say!" She whirled. "Father!"

A dismayed Harpin' John read Mr. Aaron's expression which conveyed that they were both caught between a rock and a hard place.

So Harpin' John went to hitch up the buggy, his mind racing for some answer as to how he could get away. . . for there was no way he could ignore the commands of the irate white female Melissa Anne.

The nativity pageant had been in progress for almost an hour. A mile and a half away, Fletcher Randall and the planter Tom Graves were patrolling a beat around the Randall mansion veranda, smelling the combined aromas of the pots and tubfuls of the barbecued pork, beef, veal, and chicken which were being kept in readiness along with the accompaniments of cole slaw and potato salads and dozens of sweet-potato pies, plus a liberal store of liquors and beer that would guarantee an evening never to forget.

Fletcher had convinced his mother and father that he should not attend the nativity pageant in order to remain at the mansion in case some guests also might have missed the pageant and would arrive for the Christmas Eve barbecue early. And Tom Graves had joined Fletcher just to ensure that all was going well until his valued slave Harpin' John would be able to return from playing his harmonica for Melissa Anne Aaron at the church pageant.

Two horsemen came pounding up out of the night toward the mansion, and they headed directly for the clustering of lights about the veranda. The lean, slit-eyed chief patrolman Ned Smithers swung down off his horse and came striding directly to meet the advancing Fletcher.

"Bad news, Mr. Randall. It's not what you want to hear on Christmas Eve, but there appears to be a mass escape of slaves in the making. Three are reported missing from the Aaron plantation, and it seems that six are gone from your cabins—a patrolman's checking the premises now, and trying to find out from the rest of the darkies what happened."

Fletcher could imagine the means used to extract the information. He asked, "Are you absolutely certain about this?" He hoped his dismay appeared genuine.

"About as sure as I can be, yessir. I hate to make a mess out of the senator's and your big barbecue affair here, and all-" Fletcher thought that he detected a trace of sarcasm. "But the whole thing seems to have been planned to a fare-thee-well. No telling how long they've been gone." Chief patrolman Smithers paused. "And one more thing, we're looking for Mr. Tom Graves. His wife said we'd probably find him here."

Fletcher heard Tom Graves call from behind him, "Here I am. What's the problem?"

Chief patrolman Smithers turned and nodded to his assistant, who had been standing beside his horse and now came forward, holding a bundle at his side.

Smith took the bundle, which turned out to be a brown suit-coat. He held it up to Tom Graves. "Sir, can you identify this coat?"

"Of course I can," said Tom Graves. "You see my name inked inside the collar. About a year ago I gave it to my slave, the one called Harpin' John."

Fletcher felt a sinking sensation inside his stomach.

"Where is he right now?" Smithers's tone had grown harder.

"You're asking about my slave, my property," said Tom Graves, "so I'm asking why do you want to know?"

"Well, I'll tell you. This coat was found by the patrolman who discovered the slaves were missing. It'd been left behind in one of their cabins. Question is, what was it doing there?"

"Just because you came across that damned coat doesn't mean Harpin' John had anything to do with the escape." Tom Graves was appalled at the prospect of losing a very valuable piece of property, and in truth he would also miss someone as useful and amusing as Harpin' John.

"Maybe not," Smithers said. "But I have to get hold of your slave man and ask him some hard questions, and I think we'll get some truth out of him before we finish. Where can we find him?"

"He's at the church nativity pageant," Fletcher thrust himself into the conversation. "I'll accompany you there. I think it would be best if I went in and brought him out. No need to cause a commotion in church. There'll be the devil to pay soon enough tonight. Once Harpin' John is in your hands, I'll go back and break the news to my father and all the rest."

The four men rode like the wind, and when they arrived at the church Fletcher dismounted first. "I'll be out as quickly as I can," he said, and went inside.

The nativity pageant had reached the point where the Three Wise Men, with young Parson Brown as their leader, were taking their leave of the manger where the Christ Child lay sleeping. Melissa Anne at the harpsichord was leading the background music with Harpin' John and two black slave fiddlers playing behind the performers, while the packed audience representing the planter families of the community murmured appreciatively.

When Fletcher Randall suddenly appeared in the church doorway, the reaction of Parson Brown and his companion Wise Men and Melissa Anne caused the audience to turn their heads. As Fletcher made his way briskly up the church aisle toward the stage, people stared incredulously. Fletcher passed by the front pews, in one of which sat Senator and Mrs. Randall. Their faces were disbelieving as their son stepped up onto the slightly raised stage, past Melissa Anne at her harpsichord, and went straight to black Harpin' John, who stood staring back at him, the harmonica still at his mouth.

"Follow me, *now!*" Fletcher said tautly, and turning abruptly he went double-timing to the door of the pastor's study at the church's right rear, with Harpin' John one step behind him. Once inside the small room, Fletcher asked quickly, "Your horse out back?"

"Yeah, what's happened?"

"No time to talk—" He snatched open the door to the steps outside. They could hear the first rumblings of the church audience. Fletcher barked, "Get your horse, I'll grab somebody else's."

Harpin' John grunted assent, asking no questions. People were starting to emerge from the church and he could hear chief patrolman Smithers shouting as the two horses pounded away into the darkness.

"Let's split up! Go to the place I showed you, I be there!" Harpin' John shouted to Fletcher, pulling his horse toward the right and lying low against its neck to avoid the dangerous low limbs of trees he raced past.

Within the forest, Fletcher's horse stepped into a groundhog's hole, and Fletcher tumbled off as the horse pitched forward, breaking its foreleg and screaming in pain. Fletcher struggled to his feet and then fell onto one knee. His ankle was badly hurt . . . he had never felt more alone.

But then, his chest heaving, he heard the distant hoot-owl sound. Fletcher put his hands up to his mouth, and tried his best to do what he had been taught.

The hoot-owl call in response was closer.

Harpin' John checked Fletcher's ankle. "Well, we lucky, it ain't broke. But the way it already swellin', look like a real bad sprain." He looked directly into Fletcher's face. "Wasn't sure I'd ever see you no more.

Fletcher said, "I thought you were a goner, too—"

"Would of been, hadn't been for you." Harpin' John took a long pause. "You didn't have to do what you done. How come you come in after me?"

Fletcher thought about that. "Tell you the truth, I never thought about It. I just did, that's all."

"Well, we can't rest here no longer, we got to git movin'. I know they after us, probably with dogs by now, an' we got to be either long gone or hid mighty good by daylight." Again he appraised Fletcher. "You a big man, but I can carry you to the horse, and us can both ride to a better hiding place."

Fletcher pushed himself upright again, fending away Harpin' John's help, to test himself. He tried the ankle. He winced with the pain. He managed about three hopping steps and stopped.

"It hurts. But I can make steps, especially if I lean on your shoulder. But I'd best wait lust a minute-it really hurts."

"Did they all get away?" Harpin' John asked.

"I think. It sounded like it, what little I heard."

"Well, can you tell me what happened, I mean what went wrong?"

"I sure can. You gave somebody a coat, and he left it hanging in his cabin. The patrollers found it with Tom Graves's name inside, and he told them he gave it to you."

"I be damn! You mean 'ceptin' for that, we wouldn't be out here now? All we did, and that one little thing went wrong! If I could've got out'n that pageant, I really b'lieve I'd of noticed old Uncle Ben didn't wear my coat. I should've kept it when he told me he thought it was too pretty for him to wear, anyway."

Harpin' John looked at Fletcher Randall. "Well, for sure, neither one of us can't never go back. What you goin' to do? You figured out yet where you goin'?"

"I haven't had time for that. I wasn't planning on this."

Harpin' John reflected a moment. "You know, lotsa people don't realize how many white folks risks all you got, even your lives, because you don't believe slavery's right."

Fletcher thought a little while. Then he asked, "What about you? Where are you going?"

"Jes' up North, that's all I know for now." Harpin' John chuckled. "Maybe I can start me a little business cookin' good barbecue—I can do that, an' make a little music."

Fletcher determinedly pushed himself up again. He gestured

that he was ready to try walking, with Harpin' John's assistance. Two hours later, deeper in the forest, they crossed a wide stream, and were confident they had eluded their pursuers.

Suddenly Harpin' John plucked from his pocket his harmonica, which he cupped against his mouth, and brought forth his patented resounding railroad locomotive *chuffing* sound.

Abruptly he stopped, whacking the harmonica against one knee. "Hey, lemme quit actin' a fool, 'cause you know what?" He stared up at the radiant North Star, joined by Fletcher. " 'Cause this here is Christmas morning now-won't be but a couple of hours 'fore the day breaks."

Again he raised the harmonica, saying to Fletcher, "Now here's a tune I don't know what it is, I jes' sort of remember it from hearin' it bein' played an' sung last Christmas when I was ridin' my horse amongst where some them new German emigrant peoples moved in the other end of Ashe County. I can't remember but jes' two sounds of the German words they was singin, they sounded something like '*Stille Nacht . . .* ' "

Harpin' John cupped his harmonica. "But I know the tune they played went like this."

He played. Fletcher heard the melody of "Silent Night" as the Christmas moonlight bathed the faces of the black man playing and the white man listening.

When Harpin' John finished, neither man said a word. Then the pair of them resumed walking, silhouetted against the Christmas early morning sky.

Fletcher realized that now his life had changed forever, too. He thought about his parents with a sense of pain and loss that he knew both they and he would be a long time absorbing and coming to terms with. He had made an irrevocable break with his past. He knew he had made a wreck of their lives. His father's political career would become a shambles, and in Senator Randall's eyes, indeed all Southerners' eyes, Fletcher Randall would forever be a traitor. As for his mother, she'd be devastated, and he wondered agonizingly whether she would ever recover from the shame he'd brought upon her, and from the ache of losing her only child. It would be, to both of them, as if he were dead. But whatever the ache of the present and uncertainties of his future, he knew now that by not living for himself, he was learning to live with himself, at last. He'd told Harpin' John that he wasn't sure where he'd go, or what he'd do. But he remembered one thing for sure: he had some friends in Philadelphia.

Spit in the Governor's Tea

SHAY YOUNGBLOOD
(1960-   )

Shay Youngblood was born in Columbus, Georgia, and after the
death of her mother when she was two, was raised by her aunts
and neighbors. Youngblood says that "as a child fairy tales had a
big influence on me," and she began writing when she was ten
years old. Her first book, *The Big Mama Stories* (1989), is a collection of stories told by a young woman about her "mamas," the
women who raised her after the death of her mother, "some of
the wisest women to see the light of day." Several of the stories in
this collection were adapted for the stage in the play *Shakin' The
Mess Outta Misery*, first produced by the Horizon Theatre
Company in Atlanta, Georgia (1988). Her play, *Square Blues*
(1993), written as her graduate thesis at Brown University, won
the Edward Albee Award in 1995. Youngblood drew from her
Georgia childhood to write her first novel, *Soul Kiss* (1998). She
says, "Given the disintegration of family in our communities,
many of us, including myself, must find the inner strength to go
on." Her unorthodox Christmas story, "Spit in the Governor's
Tea," was published in *The Big Mama Stories*.

$$\mathbb{T}$$

*D*ecember 1959 was the year Miss Shine got even for 400-
year-old wrongs. I was born that year, so the story was told to
me and long as I'm Black I'll never forget it. Every
Christmas Eve when Big Mama and all the other grown folks went
shopping downtown, Justine Baker would come to our apartment to
sit with me. Even though she was only in her twenties, she could tell
stories good as Aunt Mae, Big Mama, and Aunt Vi. I especially liked
the one she told me every Christmas Eve, the one bout Miss Shine.

Justine was a lil on the plump side cause she had a terrible
sweet tooth. She wore loose cotton house dresses, with pockets that

hid penny candy, and big pink curlers in her hair every day but Sunday when she sang in the choir. Her voice was soprano and real pretty so she usually had the star position in the choir stand as the soloist. I loved hearing her catch notes with her voice and then letting them fly over our heads in the congregation, like birds. When Justine was telling a story her voice was like that too-high, sweet and strong.

After I got in my red footie pajamas, brushed my teeth, and said my prayers, Justine would light Big Mama's kerosene lamp, put me in the middle of Big Mama's bed, and sit looking at me from Big Mama's rocking chair. She would fold her plump hands in her lap and rock slow, backward and forward as she told me Miss Shine's story.

"Round Christmastime there's a whole lotta things in the air you cain't see Things that make you smile at folks you don't even know and speak to your worst enemy. People get in what you call the Christmas Spirit. I'd like to think it was the Christian spirit and folks would do it every day of the year, but the world just ain't like that. This Christmas spirit infect everybody like a disease. Everything is amazement.

"Well, this particular December I'm gonna tell you bout wasn't much different. At the start of December our chorus teacher told my class we had been chose to sing Christmas carols at the governor's mansion. For weeks all the kids that lived in the projects talked bout was the school chorus singing at the governor's mansion on Christmas Eve. Glo Dean, Jimmy, Pearl, and me was all in the choir at church, too, so everybody knowed we would make our mamas proud.

"Your Big Mama was just as excited as everybody else, but when she heard she couldn't help but say out loud, 'With all the mess the governor been stirring up, standing in the schoolhouse door to keep our children from a equal education. Now the children gonna have opportunity to show him they know a lil something already."

"'Amen,'" Miss Shine broke In. "I'm gonna be there to see our children show out. The governor done asked me already to stay past sundown on Christmas Eve."

"Miss Shine had worked in the governor's mansion ever since her husband, Mr. Polk died and left her with no insurance money and a heap of bills to pay. When Mr. Polk was living, he useta cuss a mean blue streak when Miss Shine spoke bout working.

"'What you wanna work for?' he would scream, so everybody in the neighborhood could hear and know he was a man.

"'What you mean? I work every day. I near bout break my back cleaning up after you. We got bills to pay, and I want some nice things round here. Like some new curtains on the window, stead of that old sheet I sewed up so folks couldn't look in, a flower garden, and a new hat for church once in a while'.

"'Shine, where can you work? On your rusty knees in some white folks' kitchen? Bringing they nasty clothes in my house? No m'am. I ain't gonna stand for you working for white folks as long as I can swing this hammer,' he would end up, swinging his railroad hammer over his bald head.

"Mr. Polk worked on the railroad for over thirty years. When he died and couldn't swing his hammer no more, Miss Shine had to work. All she knowed was keeping house and cooking, so when Miss Emma Lou told her bout the job at the governor's mansion she ain't hesitated but a minute. Miss Shine was kinda nervous bout working in a place as fancy as the governor's mansion, but Miss Emma Lou straightened her out quick.

"'Honey chile, the governor and his wife is simple country crackers. They don't put on airs till foreigners come round. They eat, sleep, and pee out a hole just like anybody else. You member that and you'll do alright,' Miss Emma Lou said.

"'But all them fancy place settings, three or four different kinda forks and spoons, pouring tea before supper...I just don't know, Emma Lou.'

"'Colored folks, as you know, is the most amazing people on this earth. Anything we put our minds to and our hearts into, we can get done good and most times better than that. You'll never if you can do a thing till you try and a try has never failed.'

"Miss Emma Lou finished her speech by spitting in her spit cup like she always do.

"'Emma Lou, I'll do the best I kin. Thank you for the blessing.'

"Miss Shine got the job, and she caught on quick. The funniest thing she had to do was pouring tea. Every day round four o'clock the governor's wife Emmie rung a silver bell. That was Miss Shine's signal to pour boiling water in a great big silver teapot that sit on a big silver tray set with easy-to-break china cups and saucers and real silver spoons.

"Every day the governor say the same thing. 'Shine, pour me up a cupful, with round bout six spoons of sugar. I like mine sweet as Miss Emmie here'

"If there wasn't no company, Miss Emmie would crow like a rooster and say, 'Doggone if it ain't tea time again. Cheers, daddy'

"They would sit in the living room, quiet as two rocks in a river cept for the slurping of that sweet tea, for exactly thirteen minutes. Then Miss Emmie would ring her lil silver bell, and Miss Shine would either pour some more tea or roll the cart back in the kitchen. Madam Waters, the head cook would start heaping food in serving dishes, and Miss Shine would take off her white apron and start walking to the bus stop. It was a mile and a half easy. She'd wait with the other maids who worked after four o'clock for the last bus to town. From downtown she'd have to catch another bus home to the projects.

"Weeks before the first Christmas pine was chopped for decoration, Miss Shine was in charge of polishing cabinets full of silver, starching closets full of linen, and her biggest job—but the one she loved the best and saved for last—was cleaning the grand French crystal chandelier that hung in the main entry hall to the mansion. She said cleaning the 814 crystals all by hand give her time to think.

Her chandelier cleaning ritual went something like this:

"'I climb the ladder with my cleaning bucket in one hand. Once I git to the top I untwists the wire that thread through a lil bitty hole in the crystal head. The wire hold the crystal on the big brass tiered circles. I put many crystals as I kin in the bucket. Then I soaks em in ammonia and lemon juice. Then I rinses em with real hot water and lay em on clean white towel. Then I polish em with spit and a soft flannel cloth till they shine like pure diamonds.'

"Two days before the singing, a strong feeling pass over Miss Shine like something bad was bout to happen. She was sitting on top of the ladder in the entry hall taking the crystals down. She said it was like a heavy cloud press down on her and hung on her heart. She was near bout done up there so she eased down off the ladder and set up in the kitchen pantry polishing them chandelier crystals with spit and shining em with a white flannel rag. She polished the big round crystal with a thousand faces that was big as a Florida grapefruit with special care, rubbing it like she used to rub on Mr. Polk's bald head to get him to go to sleep at night. It hung from the middle of the chandelier. She spit-shined and rag-rubbed till she could see her face, that was the color of a grocery sack, in every flat edge like a mirror.

"Christmas Eve day the snow started falling round noon. Fat white flakes covered the ground like one of Aunt Judy's wedding quilts. The governor and his family invited some friends and neighbors over to the mansion to have a early supper. Just as they was finishing they meal, the three yellow school buses rolled round the circle driveway and parked on the side in the bus parking spaces. The governor, Miss Emmie, and they few friends went out on the front porch to watch the first group assemble round that twenty-five-foot Christmas tree all decorated and lit up in the middle of that lawn all covered with snow. Miss Shine dried her hands on her apron and stood in the front window looking out from behind the curtains, her heart near bout busting with joy. She knowed we was gonna do her proud that night.

"The first group of them white children sang they Christmas carols in high-pitched cut-off notes that didn't sound right to us, nor Miss Shine, but she clapped when they was done with 'Jingle Bells,' 'We Wish You a Merry Christmas,' and 'White Christmas,' even though they messed up them songs like broke glass on bicycle tires.

"The second group wasn't much better. They was from a church-run school, so they sang a lot of hymns. Like the first group, every one of em was white and dressed just alike in blue jackets, with pants for the boys and skirts for the girls. Miss Shine wasn't impressed, but she clapped for them, too.

"Then us colored children broke loose. We arranged ourselves round that Christmas tree, holding hands in a circle. We was wearing long white robes with gold sashes over our shoulders looking like black angels. Miss Shine felt faint. 'Oh Come All Ye Faithful', 'Away In a Manger', 'Oh Holy Night', and just when she thought she couldn't take no more heavenly sounds, I led the choir in 'Silent Night.' When I was done there was a deep hush, quiet like even God had stopped what She was doing to listen. I was feeling the spirit cause God was leading that song. Miss Shine almost forgot where she was. She clapped long and loud, put her hand over her heart, and kept clapping on her hip with her free hand even when we was heading for our bus. She could see Glo Dean, Jimmy, Pearl, me, and the others dancing round that tree like we was at home round the chinaberry tree in July.

"The governor went out on the lawn as we was gathering near our separate buses. I remember it clear as day. The governor's speech went something like this:

"'That was some real nice caroling children. You all did a fine job. How bout another round of applause for everybody.'

"He said *everybody* like it hurt him, then he said, 'I would like to take this opportunity to invite Middle T. Morris School and St. Joseph's Academy to join my wife and myself and our guests in the mansion for a cup of hot chocolate. That was some mighty fine singing from my alma mater and rival school. Come on in children.

Merry Christmas to you.'

"He waved the white children over to the front door and welcomed them with a handshake into the entry hall of the mansion.

"Something inside of Miss Shine broke in two when she saw our faces. Glo Dean and the others looked soft and sad like they was gonna cry. Jimmy's face was hard, like he wanted to pitch a brick through the front windows of the mansion. Pearl looked like she didn't spect no less. I was just too shame to look anywhere but down at the ground. I couldn't believe that after he heard God in my song he could be so mean and cold-hearted.

"Miss Emmie rushed into the entry hall and found Miss Shine still as a stature standing at the window staring at the white children lining up at the door and the colored bus pulling outta sight down the driveway.

"'Shine, quick, fix the children some hot chocolate. There seems to be bout thirty-five of em. Not too much sugar now, or the lambs will be up all night,' Miss Emmie said, sweet as Brer Fox in the briar patch.

"Miss Shine walked to the kitchen with lead feet, like a woman without her mind. She fixed the hot chocolate rattling pots and pans, dropping the silver, and spilling milk all over the floor. She was madder than a foam-mouth dog, but what could she do? She poured the hot chocolate into thirty-five white dixie cups for thirty-five thin pink lips to drink from. Her hands was trembling and her head felt light. Her blood pressure was rising. She kept thinking that they was all just children. Why couldn't the governor see that? Color don't matter in the sight of God. The governor think he know more than God?

"When all the cups was full and on the rolling tea cart, Miss Shine, pushed it slow into the entry hail. She heard one of the white kids say something bout *sending the niggers back to the jungle* and heard laughing break out round the room and saw wide grins on the governor and Miss Emmie's faces. Each one of em took a cup without even a thank you or a look in Miss Shine's direction.

She left it in the Lord's hands, and She come through. With no warning, the big round crystal that hung from the middle of the chandelier fell with a loud crack on the marble floor, breaking into a million pieces. Miss Shine's mouth dropped open and her eyes got big. It didn't hurt nobody, but she took it to be a sign.

"'Them niggers must've sent a voodoo in here on us,' one of the girls said, giggling nervouslike. Miss Shine fixed a look on that chile that made her turn red as a beet and start to cry.

"Miss Emmie seen Miss Shine staring at that chile and snapped up, 'Shine get a broom and sweep up this mess before one of these children gets hurt.'

"She was trying to break Miss Shine's spell on the child, and she did, but Miss Shine turned to stare Miss Emmie full in the face for a long uncomfortable minute before going back in the kitchen.

"Miss Shine come back and parted the crowd with the point of her broom, waving it wild, just missing knocking a few blond heads and poking out a few blue eyes. She swept up every sliver of crystal she could find. Then she put the pieces in a paper sack. After collecting all the empty cups and cleaning up the kitchen, she walked that mile and a half through the snow to a main street. She hailed a taxi that took her home. The streets was mostly empty, as it was near nine o'clock. It was cold and snow was still falling.

"When she got in her apartment she turned the oven on and opened the door to warm up the kitchen. Then she pulled out a chair and stood on it. She felt round up on the top kitchen shelf for a fat white candle she had bought at a spiritual store years before for the purpose of a ritual Miss Mary told her to do, but she never did. She sat down with it at the kitchen table, still in her coat dripping with snow. She lit the candle and sit there staring at it. She poured the broke up crystal from the paper sack onto a piece of newspaper spread out on the table and looked at em while talking to herself. Them pieces of crystal still sparkled like diamonds, but every jagged edge was like a dagger in her heart. Miss Shine sit at her kitchen table till Christmas morning broke light sit there till the thing she had to do come to her.

"'Folks say things changed, but it's still like slavery times.' Miss Shine's mind eased way, way back. She heard a chant far off, deep as slave graves and old as Africa.

"*Blood boiled thick, run red like a river, slaves scream, wail, moan after their dead. Daddy lynched, mama raped, baby sister sold down river. Slaves scream, wail, moan after their dead. The cook know what to do to save the race, stop the screams, save the blood from boiling thick, running red like a river.*

"Miss Shine all of a sudden knowed what she had to do to save the race. It come to her like in a dream, but it was real. It was a story told to her a long time ago. In slavery times the cook had a heap of power. They stole food to feed the children to keep em from dying before they was sold off. Fed the mens scraps of lean meat to give em the strength to find freedom and bring it back home The cook had the power to poison the master, too. When the beatings, killings, and selling off of families was too much to bear, often time the cook would use her knowledge of herbs and roots to make her white master sick, sometimes die.

"Miss Shine was possessed by her power. She snatched off her coat and white apron and went into her bedroom to get the wood bowl her mama give her and the iron head of Mr. Polk's hammer. She came back to the table spread with all that broke crystal and ground it up with the head of the hammer in her mama's wood bowl. She ground it till sweat dripped off her face into the bowl. She ground it till the crystals was fine as dust and tied the pile of it in a corner of her slip. She burnt the bowl in her tin bathtub and flushed the ashes down the toilet. Then she wrapped the hammer-head in flannel and put it away.

"*Nobody know how the master get sick. Nobody know how he die. The doctors won't know why he pain so in his stomach. The grind be so fine. He think it be root work and be scared of niggers from then on.* The cooks kept whispering in her ears, chanting.

"When Miss Shine had to go back to work after New Year's, she was ready, almost happy. All the other women on the maids' bus was grumbling bout having to go back to work.

"'Somebody got to pay them bill collectors,' a voice in the back of the bus hollered out. That put everybody in a good mood, Miss Shine was really wanting to get to the mansion that morning.

"Miss Emmie stopped her from washing the lunch dishes to tell her they was having a guest to dinner and he was gonna have tea with em. Miss Shine *yes m'amed* her, looking direct in her eyes. Miss Emmie wasn't used to coloreds making eye contact and she near bout run out the kitchen. Miss Shine went on as usual fixing tea. She put the kettle on to boil.

"*Blood boilt thick . . .*

"She kept hearing the whispers. She poured the boiling water over the tea leaves and strained it into the big silver teapot

"*Run red like a raging river...*

"She took down three china cups with a flower pattern and set em straight on matching saucers.

"*Nobody know how the master get sick...*

"Miss Shine put everything on the big tea cart.

"*Nobody know how he die...*

"She untied the knot in the corner of her slip, emptied the powder into the sugar bowl, and stirred it up good.

"*You done good sister. . . you done right. . . we can rest now...* That was the last whisper.

"Miss Shine smile before she serve the governor, Miss Emmie, and they stone-face guest a south Georgia mayor with a beer belly and a mouth full of *nigras*. Miss Shine kept pouring tea for the governor and Miss Emmie for more than two weeks before she disappeared.

"Some folks say she move to a entirely colored town in Texas. Other folks say she wasn't really of this world in the first place. Nobody living ever see Miss Shine again. She told me this story the day Aunt Judy sent me to her house with a piece of Christmas cake, two days before she disappeared.

"The doctor that examined the governor couldn't find nothing wrong with him. As delicate as she look, Miss Emmie musta had a iron stomach, she wasn't but a lil bit sick. The governor suffered stomach pains for the rest of his life. He got cancer of the intestines at the age of seventy-two and died after a long and painful sickness.

"From then on, the school chorus started singing Christmas carols at the colored nursing home every year to honor our own folk. Nobody never talk bout wanting to sing for the governor no more. Every time I sing 'The Spirit Can Move' solo, I dedicate it to Miss Shine, wherever she is. Always remember your ancestors."

Gift Rap

TERRY KAY
(1938–   )

Terry Winter Kay, named for the Terry Winter apple, was born the
eleventh of twelve children on a farm in Hart County, Georgia.
Kay says, "I grew up in a loving home, and have none of the
expected southern dysfunctional family stories to tell about my
childhood." In 1959 he began his journalism career at a weekly
newspaper in Decatur, Georgia, and then worked for *The Atlanta
Journal,* first as a sports writer and later as their film and theater
reviewer. Kay wrote his first novel, *The Year the Lights Came On*
(1976), at the insistence of his friend Pat Conroy, who believed in
his talent for fiction. Both authors were part of the birth of a contemporary literary culture in Atlanta, centered at Cliff Graubart's
Old New York Bookshop. Kay's second novel, *After Eli* (1981),
set in the North Georgia Mountains, was written in response to
James Dickey's *Deliverance.* His other works include *Dark Thirty*
(1984), *To Dance with the White Dog* (1990), *To Whom the Angel
Spoke* (1991), *The Runaway* (1997), and *The Kidnapping of
Aaron Greene* (1999). The best-selling *To Dance with the White
Dog* was produced by Hallmark Hall of Fame in 1993. Kay has
written numerous screenplays, including the Emmy-Award winning *Run Down the Rabbit.* Proud to be called a Southern writer,
Kay contends that, "The best writing has always come from the
South." He points to Erskine Caldwell's *The Sacrilege of Alan
Kent* as having a tremendous influence on him. Kay says, "I read
it when I was about eighteen or nineteen, and not knowing it
then, I picked up a lot of what I now refer to as a sense of power
in words." Kay's own "sense of power in words," can be seen not
only in his fiction, but his nonfiction as well. For several years he
was a contributing editor of *Atlanta Magazine,* and as critic-at-
large wrote commentary on a wide range of subjects, including
"Gift Rap (1992)," his thoughts on the commercialization of
Christmas.

The best memory I have of Christmas, as a parent, was the evening that my oldest daughter—then a one-year-old—pulled a wrapped package beneath the tree two days earlier than Santa Claus would have liked, and proceeded to rip it open.

Inside the package was a doll, a squint-eyed thing that I considered on-purpose, new-born-baby ugly. I had protested to my wife that it would cause nightmares or even more severe traumas. My complaints were ignored with a stare that said, "This is a mother-daughter thing."

Of course, she was right. My daughter's face was radiant when she tore open the box.

"Baby," she whispered in awe. "Baby." She held it to her face, like a mother being tender with her child.

That doll became Lucy, and from that Christmas until she was lost on a trip many years later, Lucy was always within reach of my daughter. The tears of woe over that sad mishap were so great, I have spent almost thirty years trying to duplicate Lucy in flea markets and doll shops.

My daughter had cried, "There's only one Lucy."

After all these years, I believe her.

Point is, shopping for Christmas toys is not an easy task, especially today.

The choices are too many, too appealing.

Used to be—or so memory tells me—it was as simple as a walk-through in a five-and-dime store.

Boys got something from the sports table, or toy pistols, or toy cars. Maybe some Tinker-toys, or pick-up sticks. Maybe even a Red Ryder BB rifle.

Girls got dolls, and other stuff. I don't know what, make-believe makeup kits, maybe. Imitation jewelry. I didn't pay very much attention.

No one fretted that what was being given would be sneered at, or refused, or ignored. A gift was something, and something was considerably better than nothing.

Not so today.

Today, everyone seems to want a toy that is popular, safe, educational, durable, relatively inexpensive, and one that ranks high on the Child Delight Meter.

The only thing I know that comes close to meeting the above requisites is a large cardboard shipping box:

Popular—How many of us have watched children tear open a gift, turn it over a couple of times, toss it away, and pick up the box it came in?

Safe—Sure, youngsters can get hurt playing with, or in, boxes, but chances are the toy inside the box is far more dangerous.

Educational—With boxes, children must use their imagination. Does a greater instrument of education exist than the imagination?

Durable—Boxes are like good dogs around children. They can take the punishment and still be there.

Relatively inexpensive—How much can a box cost in comparison to the gift it holds?

Child Delight Meter—Refer to "popular" and "educational" items above, or better yet, refer to experience.

In addition, a box does not require batteries, which are never included when they should be included. It does not need late-night home assembly with directions that not even the CIA could follow. It can be drawn on with Magic Marker and become magical. And when it is finally crushed from the weight of imagination—from being submarines and spaceships, dollhouses and dark caves—it may be recycled for such mundane purposes as holding items for sale. It is even biodegradable for those too casual to recycle.

Yet, to my knowledge, no one makes cardboard shipping boxes for the express purpose of functioning as a toy, and in that decision or oversight is a statement about our values that is worth pondering:

If we get a wrapped box, we expect something other than possibility to be inside it.

Still, like most shoppers, I enjoy the annual dilemma of the what and how many of Christmas toys, and then the rushing-around search to find them at a slashed-price deal. (And I am referring only to children's toys, not that gaudy nonsense annually advertised for over-rich adults. A Mercedes golf cart? May it dogleg left and find the fairway to hell.)

An investigative tour of one of the Toys "R" Us stores is a trip into a latter-day land of fantasy. Little wonder the corporate powers that be are building twenty-five-thirty of these toy-stacked emporiums each year in America. They know that cash flow is bound to follow the squeal of childish joy.

We used to be happy with a simple game of checkers. Now they have a board that can be used for checkers, chess, backgammon, Parcheesi, Chinese checkers and something called Chutes & Ladders.

The standards are still available, but they're often hard to recognize.

The toy truck we once pushed around in the back yard has now been upgraded by Tonka to the size of a riding lawn mower.

The roller skate is now an in-line skate, or something called a Rollerblade.

You can now buy a kite that looks like a fighter plane and has electronic battling sounds.

And I swear there are bicycles with more gears than spokes in the wheels.

Barbie, the doll's doll, is still as youthful and fetching as Brenda Starr, and still on the shelves, but she's a modern woman of action. She can be found in a Patio Party box, or a Backyard Cookout box, or a Sunshine Holiday box, and a few other places where the energetic gather. She is even featured in a wedding dress, which makes me wonder if she's managed to trap Ken at the altar. Oh, yes, Ken's still around. Still smiling, the little devil that he is. Personally, I think he's got his eye on Midge, Barbie's best friend.

And the Cabbage Patch Kids are plentiful. My favorite is the one called Newborn (but it's not Lucy). It is advertised with a "magical monitor," and it "cries, giggles, and calls 'Ma Ma.'" Cute, real cute.

But there always seems to be a head-liner Christmas gift, and, if the pleading of my oldest grandson—son of Lucy's mother—is an indicator, that gift would have to be from Nintendo.

The Nintendo games are advertised as the World of Nintendo. There's no brag in the claim. It is a world. Strange. Baffling. And every year, something new.

That, of course, is the key to toy manufacturing: Keep it coming with upgraded and improved product. The new look, the new appeal. It's a little like adults who collect Christmas plates from Hummel. If it's another year, there's another edition.

According to Matt Dodge, the assistant inventory control manager for the Southeast region of Toys "R" Us, the key to the business of toys is "...always to keep fresh."

Dodge admits that even Nintendo has leveled off over the years, but, "...they keep bringing out new generations of software, offering new and more exciting games."

Dodge must be right. My grandson tells me the same thing, insisting that he will be considered the neighborhood oddball if he can't have his fingers flying over the latest Nintendo challenge.

He thinks I am a sucker for his woeful expression. He is right.

But all of this is the *business* of toys, which doesn't necessarily have anything to do with the *spirit* of toys. The spirit touches the heart, not the wallet.

In his book *Without Reservations*, Fred Alias presents a story about a hotel clerk who was shopping one day in a thrift store and overheard a small girl begging her mother for a doll's house that was in need of repair. The mother tried to explain that there was no money for dollhouses, that a winter coat was more important.

The hotel clerk followed the mother and child when they left the store, noting their address. He then went back to the thrift shop, purchased the dollhouse and spent his spare time repairing it. On Christmas Eve, he tied a bow around the dollhouse and delivered it in the middle of the night to the front steps of the home where the girl lived.

Forgive me for being sentimental, but I like that story. It reminds that there are things that can't be purchased in Toys "R" Us, or any other shop.

And I think it confirms something that's important at Christmas: A doll's house given out of caring is more valuable than diamonds—if your heart is the heart of a child. If it isn't, you will never understand what giving, or receiving, really means, anyway.

from "A Lesson Before Dying"

ERNEST J. GAINES
(1933–   )

Ernest J. Gaines was born the eldest of eleven children on a plantation in Pointe Coupee Parish near New Roads, Louisiana, which is the Bayonne of all his fictional works. Like his father, Gaines worked in plantation fields until he was fifteen, when he moved to live with his mother and stepfather in Vallejo California. It was here that Gaines began reading voraciously, trying to learn all he could about rural blacks in the South. Unable to find books that he felt honestly portrayed the life of blacks in the South, Gaines wrote a novel at the age of sixteen in an attempt to fill this void. Rejected by publishers, he put the manuscript away. Gaines enrolled at San Francisco State College in 1955, began publishing stories in 1956, and received the Joseph Henry Jackson Award for his story "Comeback" in 1959. Following his Wallace Stegner Creative Writing Fellowship at Stanford in 1959, Gaines led a bohemian life style in San Francisco and devoted his days to writing. Gaines worked on the manuscript he had put away at age sixteen, and published it under the title *Catherine Carmier* (1964). With the publication of *The Autobiography of Miss Jane Pittman* (1971), Gaines earned critical acclaim. In 1983, Gaines became writer-in-residence at the University of Southwestern Louisiana. True to his past, Gaines' latest novel, *A Lesson Before Dying* (1993), focuses on life in Louisiana and the violence that blacks faced as slaves and free men. The novel won the Southern Book Critics Circle Award for the best work of fiction of the year. In this excerpt from *A Lesson Before Dying*, Gaines writes of a children's Christmas pageant in a rural Louisiana community in the late 1940s.

𝓘t was cold and it rained for the two weeks preceding our Christmas program. It rained too much for the people to go out into the field to cut cane, and the field and the roads were too muddy for the cane to be brought to the derrick for loading and then shipment to the mill for grinding. People stayed at home around the fireplace or near the stove in the kitchen. You could see gray-blue smoke rising from the big chimneys in the fronts of the houses and from the smaller chimneys in the backs. And because the wind always came into the quarter from the river this time of year, you could see the smoke drifting from the quarter back across the field toward the cemetery and the swamp. The only time you were likely to see someone out in the yard was to cut more wood to throw onto the fireplace or put into the kitchen stove. The rest of the time, the quarter was deserted, the doors and windows shut tight against the cold wind and the rain.

There was still a light drizzle on the night of the program, but it did not keep the people away. I had told the students that this program should be dedicated to Jefferson, and they had taken the message home, and many people who had never attended a Christmas or graduation program came to the church that night. The program began at seven o'clock, but people were there much earlier. Because of the rain, they could not drive cars in the quarter, so they either walked or came by wagon. Reverend Ambrose, who lived up the river and not on the plantation, parked his car along the highway and walked to the church. As usual, he was dressed in a dark suit, white shirt, and dark tie, but tonight he also wore a yellow slicker. Most of the other people wore their "going-to-town" clothes. Not their everyday working clothes, and not their Sunday best either. Going-to-town clothes were old clothes, but without any visible patches. The shirts and the dresses may have been faded, but they were clean and they were neat.

No one lingered outside, as they would have had the weather been better. After scraping off their shoes on the bottom step, they kicked the mud on the ground and came inside the church. The womenfolks who had brought food set their pots or pans or bowls on the tables that we had placed against the blackboards in the back. Mrs. Sarah James, who had arrived at six-thirty, sat guarding the food until after the program, when everyone would eat. The other women took vacant seats as close to the heater as they could get. The men and the older boys stood in the back, talking, until the womenfolks told them to sit down.

I was behind the curtain with the students who had been chosen to participate in the Christmas play. The curtain was made up of four bedsheets, suspended from a wire that extended from one side of the church to the other. Three of the sheets were very white; the fourth was a light gray. This one belonged to Miss Rita Lawrence, and as long back as I could remember, she had insisted on contributing something to the Christmas program, and every time it was a sheet, probably the same one, and it was never as white as the others. The audience always knew which sheet was Miss Rita's, and they thought it was embarrassing to have it hanging up there with all the others, but no one had the courage to speak to Miss Rita about it and each year it was one of the four that made up the curtain.

Irene Cole and Odessa Freeman were assisting me in preparing the students behind the curtain. The two shepherds wore brown crokersacks over their dress clothes, and each of them carried a tall bamboo cane curved at the top and tied with black thread. The three wise men wore crepe-paper robes. The robes were red, green, and yellow. Irene and Odessa continued to remind the wise men to be careful not to tear their robes by moving around so much. Mary, the mother of Jesus, wore a wrinkled blue denim dress to show that she was a poor woman. Joseph, her husband, had on overalls and carried a hammer in the loop of his pants. Baby Jesus was a white alabaster doll dressed in a long white gown. The girls in the choir wore white dresses, the boys white shirts.

Every so often I would part the curtain to see how many people had come in. Miss Rita Lawrence and her big grandson, Bok, were two of the first people there and sat up front, with Bok taking up almost a third of the bench. Twice Bok had been sent to the mental institution at Jackson, but the doctors there knew he was not dangerous and felt they could do no more for him than Miss Rita probably could do for him at home, and after keeping him a week or two they sent him back to her. Bok had one peculiarity other than being unable to look after himself, and that was his love for marbles. He carried them with him all the time. He sat there now, playing with the marbles in the right pocket of his overalls. Miss Rita occasionally had to touch him on the hand to keep them quiet.

On the bench with Bok and Miss Rita sat Julia Lavonia, who had two children in the program, the boy as one of the shepherds, and the girl as Mary, mother of Jesus. James, her husband, was not there. A short, big-headed mulatto with curly black hair and gray eyes, he had told me once that he had better things to do than go to a coon gathering. But Julia was there, and I knew that she had brought pecan and coconut pralines, just as she did every year. The Freemans had come in too. Joe Freeman sat far in the back, but his wife, Harriet, and her mother, Aunt Agnes, and several of the children were up front, directly behind Miss Rita, Bok, and Julia Lavonia. The Coles, Irene's People, sat behind them—Norman and his wife, Sarah, Sarah's mother, Lelia Wells, Sarah's sister, Esther, and Esther's boyfriend, Henry, and two or three children. Sarah usually brought crackling and baked sweet potatoes to the Christmas program.

On the other side of the aisle, in the front row, and still wearing their overcoats because they were far from the heater, sat my aunt and Miss Emma, Miss Eloise Bouie and Inez. Behind them were Farrell Jarreau and his little wife, Ofelia. Ofelia was a delicate mulatto woman whose sisters came to the plantation every Sunday morning to take her to the Catholic church in Bayonne. She would return late in the evening, and we would hardly see her again until the next Sunday, when she would climb into the back of the car to go to mass. I supposed it was her husband, Farrell, who got her out tonight, because she had never come before. Behind them sat most of the Martin family—about ten of them—most, but not all. The father, Herbert, was not there, and neither was the idiot boy, Jesse, or the pregnant daughter, Vera, or the old grandmother. But Viola, the mother, was there, along with eight or nine of her children. Two others were in the choir, behind the curtain. The Williamses were there—four of them; three Ruffins—mother, son, and daughter— were there. The Griffins, Harry and Lena, with their two grown-up unmarried daughters, Alberda and Louberda, were there. So the church was nearly full, and it was only a quarter to seven. The bad weather had not kept them away but probably had brought them out tonight. Since they could not work in the field or in their gardens, they had no reason to stay at home, claiming to be tired.

At seven o'clock I parted the curtains and stepped out to face the audience. I told them how happy the children and I were to see them all here tonight and that I knew they would enjoy the program because their children had worked so hard the past weeks to make it a success. I invited Reverend Ambrose, who sat in one of the side pews, to lead us in prayer. He stood and asked all to stand and bow their heads. The Lord's Prayer was first. Then he thanked God for letting us see a brand-new day and for allowing us to gather together in His house in such inclement weather. (The minister was a small man and seemed timid, but he did possess a strong, demanding voice when he prayed.) He asked God to go with all the sick and afflicted, both at home and in the hospitals across this land. He asked God to visit the jail cells all over the land and especially in Bayonne and to go with the guilty and the innocent. He asked God to go with all those here tonight who did not know Him in the pardon of their sins and thought they did not need Him. No matter how educated a man was (he meant me, though he didn't call my name), he, too, was locked in a cold, dark cell of ignorance if he did not know God in the pardon of his sins. He closed by beseeching God to look down upon this humble little church and bless this gathering.

The people responded with "Amen" and sat back down. My aunt said "Amen" louder than anyone, and she was looking directly at me.

I went behind the curtain and, taking one of the middle sheets while a student did the same on the other side, pulled the curtain back to reveal the stage. The choir of a dozen boys and girls moved down below the altar to sing "Silent Night." Irene Cole directed them. I stood behind the gathered curtain on the right so that I could watch both the choir and the audience.

The children had worked hard, and they sang beautifully — and this, too, was due to the bad weather. At any other time they would have had to go home to work in the field or around the house. But since the weather had been so inclement — to use one of Reverend Ambrose's words — they had had more time for practice. The audience appreciated the singing. Even those who did not respond with "Amen, Amen" gave the choir their closest attention. So did Bok. Once he raised his hand to point, a sign to show how affected he was by the singing, but Miss Rita took the hand gently and brought it to his knee. She kept her hand on his, not pressing it, but comforting him.

After "Silent Night," the choir sang "O Little Town of Bethlehem," and my eyes left the audience, and I looked at the little pine tree stuck in the tub of dirt, decorated with strips of red and green crepe paper and bits of lint cotton and streamers of tinsel and a little white cardboard star on its highest branch. And under the tree and propped against the tub was one lone gift, wrapped in red paper and tied with a green ribbon and with a red and green bow. The children had contributed nickels, dimes, quarters — money they had made from picking pecans — and Irene, Odessa, and Odeal James had gone to Baton Rouge and bought a wool sweater and a pair of wool socks.

The people sitting up front could see the package, and they knew who it was for, and at times I could see their eyes shifting from the choir toward the tree, and I could see the change in their expressions.

But "Jingle Bells," a gayer and livelier song than the previous two, brought everyone's attention back to the choir, and I could catch in people's faces relief from their thoughts.

Odessa Freeman's "'Twas the Night before Christmas" followed, and it was more than a simple recitation; it was a dramatic performance. In her long white dress with long sleeves, and with her black hair, recently straightened and shining, combed back and tied with a white silk ribbon, and her body swaying, and her arms spread out one moment, then closed so that the palms of her hands came together, and her voice rising to fill the church, then falling to a whisper that you could barely hear—Odessa not only made you see the room where the stockings were hung, but enabled you to hear the reindeer on the roof and hear Santa before you saw him come down the chimney to fill the stockings. You heard him call the name of each reindeer after ascending the chimney, and you actually watched the reindeer going to the next house in the quarter. It was so real that Bok felt it too and pointed again, and Miss Rita nodded that she understood his feeling, and she drew back the hand and placed it on his knee and kept her own hand on his to comfort him.

Following the poem came an essay, "The Little Pine Tree," written and read by Albert H. Martin III. He told of all the other Christmas trees over the years—of oak, of cypress, of strange bushes that could not be named. He told of how the trees had been cut in the pasture and dragged back to the quarter and how the girls had washed the leaves to make the tree presentable. Then he came to the little pine tree: not a great tree—it was not tall, not blessed with great limbs—but it was pine, and it was the most beautiful of all the Christmas trees. The little pine tree even took on a character of its own, it was so happy to be here. While he spoke, Albert Martin III gestured toward the tree, and everybody looked at the tree and at the single gift underneath it.

"Hark! the Herald Angels Sing" came next, and led into the nativity scene. As the song ended, two shepherds in their crocker-sack robes came onstage behind the choir. The shepherds were attending their flock, when suddenly a light appeared on the back wall under the pictures of Christ and Reverend Ambrose. The light came from a flashlight held by a student from stage right.

Shepherd One: (Pointing) A star in the east.

Shepherd Two: And so bright.

Shepherd One: What does it mean?

Shepherd Two: Wish I knowed.

(Shepherd One looked at Shepherd Two as if he were about to correct his grammar, but changed his mind. No one in the audience seemed to have noticed.)

Three wise men enter from stage right, dressed in red, green, and yellow robes of crepe paper. (Several people in the audience snickered and made comments.)

Shepherd One: Wise men. They can tell us.

Shepherd Two: Tell us, O wise men. What yon star mean?

Wise Man One: It shines down on Bethlehem.

Wise Man Two: Little town of Bethlehem.

Wise Man Three: We must go to Bethlehem.

They all look at the star. (The star moved a little, as if the person holding the flashlight was getting tired.)

Shepherd One: But what it mean?

Wise Man One: In time you will know.

Shepherd Two: How we go'n know?

Wise Man One: He'll let us know.

Shepherd One: God on high?

Wise Man One: Works in mysterious way.

(The light moved again, as if the person was changing hands or giving the flashlight to someone else to hold.)

Wise Man Two: Wonders to perform.

Shepherd Two: But we ain't nothing but poor little old shepherds.

Wise Man One: The lowest is highest in His eyes.

Wise Man Two: Let us be off.

Wise Man Three: To yon Bethlehem.

The wise men leave stage right.

Shepherd One: Brightest star I ever seen.

Shepherd Two: Got to mean something

(The star dipped down and came back up. Shepherd One looked at the person holding the light, and looked back at me to be sure I had seen it too.)

Shepherd One: Let us kneel down. Nothing will bother the flock tonight.

The shepherds kneel as the curtain closes. The curtain opens immediately afterward. We see Mary sitting on a bench holding baby Jesus. Joseph stands beside her, looking down upon the baby. A hammer hangs from Joseph's overall loop. Offstage right, people are heard approaching.

First Speaker: The star points yon.

Second Speaker: We close now.

Third Speaker: Yon. Yon. The stable.

The three wise men enter from stage right and immediately kneel down before Mary and baby Jesus.

Wise Man One: Surely, He come.

Wise Man Two: (Nodding) Him, all right.

Wise Man Three: Our Savior.

All Three: We bring Thee gifts, O Lord. (Each places a penny on the bench beside Mary.)

Mary: (Surprised) My little baby? Savior?

Wise Man One: (Nodding) Your little baby.

Mary: (Happy) My little baby. (She holds Him up to Joseph.) Look, Joseph. My little baby. Savior.

Joseph nods but does not speak.

Mary, rocking baby Jesus in her arms, begins to sing "Joy to the

World, the Lord is come." The wise men stand and join her, and so does Joseph and the shepherds and the choir and all the others, including the boy who held the flashlight. As the song ends, they all bow to the audience.

While the children remained onstage, I asked Reverend Ambrose if he had any last remarks. Again he thanked God for allowing so many people to come out tonight. Again he reminded us that we were not all saved from sin. Even with book learning, we were still fools if we did not have God in our hearts. Again he asked God to go with those locked up in prison cells. He thanked God for all his blessings. And the congregation responded with "Amen, Amen, Amen."

I thanked the minister and told the congregation that that was our program for this year, and I reminded them that there were refreshments in the back.

The children waited onstage to hear what I thought of the program. I told them that it was fine, just fine. The children the stage to get in line for food.

"Do you want me to bring you something, Mr. Wiggins?" Irene asked me.

"No, thanks," I said.

"Something the matter, Mr. Wiggins?"

"No. Why?" I said.

"You don't look too happy."

"I'm okay," I said. "Go on and get something to eat."

Irene left to get in line, but she looked back at me over her shoulder.

She was right; I was not happy. I had heard the same carols all my life, seen the same little play, with the same mistakes in grammar. The minister had offered the same prayer as always, Christmas or Sunday. The same people wore the same old clothes and sat in the same places. Next year it would be the same, and the year after that, the same again. Vivian said things were changing. But where were they changing?

I looked back at the people around the tables, talking, eating, drinking their coffee and lemonade. But I was not with them. I stood alone.

I saw one of the little Hebert girls coming up the aisle toward me, balancing a napkin of food on both her hands. She had to pass by the tree before reaching the pulpit. She watched the food all the time to be sure she did not drop anything.

"Miss Lou say bring you this."

"Thanks, Gloria."

I sat on a chair inside the pulpit, eating fried chicken and bread. The people were still laughing and talking. Just outside the pulpit was the little pine Christmas tree with its green and red strips of crepe paper for lights, its bits of lint cotton for snow, and the narrow strings of tinsel for icicles. And there was the lone gift against the tub of dirt.

from "Dori Sanders' Country Cooking"

DORI SANDERS
(1934–   )

Dori Sanders was born the eighth of ten children in York County, South Carolina, and raised on one of the oldest black-owned farms in the state. While she was growing up in the small town of Filbert, it consisted of a general store, a peach packing shed, cotton gin, two churches, two schools and a depot. Her father was the principal of a small elementary school, and her mother coached her children in *a capella* singing. Reflecting upon her childhood, Sanders says, "Books were also a necessity of life to us. I grew up with Homer, Hawthorne and other classics." Sanders took classes at American University in Washington, D.C., but returned to her roots to help run the family farm, harvesting Georgia Belle and Elberta peaches with her brothers and sisters, and operating the Sanders peach shed during growing season. While working in the shed one day, Sanders glimpsed a slow-moving funeral procession down Highway 321, and it made her imagination soar, resulting in her writing her first novel, *Clover* (1990). Sanders received the Lillian Smith Award for fiction for *Clover* in 1992, and the book was made into a movie for cable television in 1997. She published a second novel, *Her Own Place* (1993). Sanders says that when her family is working on the farm, "we find ourselves talking about the past, and what we seem to remember most is the food." Drawing from those memories, Sanders wrote *Dori Sanders' Country Cooking* (1995). Memories of Aunt Vestula are the fondest in the Sanders family, and her ideas for celebrating Christmas are given in "Christmas Decorations" and "The Christmas Give," excerpted from the cookbook. Sanders says, "I hope that this collection of recipes and memories will take you back . . . to a world of old-fashioned family cooking and Southern country warmth and hospitality."

CHRISTMAS DECORATIONS

*A*unt Vestula decorated our house for the holidays with the same ritualistic fervor as when she cooked. She would get my daddy to cut a perfect cone-shaped cedar tree and bring it into the living room. First she placed a wisp of field cotton near the base of each branch. Nobody else in Filbert, South Carolina, put their cotton on the tree that way. Everybody else put it on the outer tips of the branches, but Aunt Vestula tucked it all the way down by the trunk. Next she went outdoors and gathered small branches from other cedar trees, choosing those with the most dusty, silvery-blue cedar berries. She would tie these little branches onto the tree, along with pinecones and some sprigs of holly with glossy spiky leaves and bright red berries. Then she would take short lengths of old, used lace—never longer than a yard—and drape them over a few branches. She would cover the ends of the lace with big bows made of white crepe paper, shredding the streamers that trailed from the bows with a fork to make ribbons. For the finishing touch Aunt Vestula polished dried honey locust pods to a beautiful mahogany color, threaded them onto a string and festooned the branches with them. My sister Virginia follows this tradition to this day.

Aunt Vestula placed additional sprays of cedar branches, pinecones, and holly with berries all over the house—on and above the mantle, in every window, and even in small wooden kegs. Finally, Aunt Vestula tied streamers cut from crisply starched gingham and calico cloth around the stair railings, with bows attached here and there from top to bottom, a custom she brought from South Carolina's Low Country where she worked. Only then was the house ready for the holidays.

THE CHRISTMAS GIVE

*a*unt Vestula and my grandparents provided us with many traditions. One of my favorites was the "Christmas give." By this tradition, you knocked on your friends' doors during the Christmas season, and as soon as the door opened a crack, you yelled "Christmas give!"

Sometimes children would yell it out as soon as they heard someone coming to answer the door, but by the rules you were supposed to wait until the door began to open. Anyway, nine times out of ten you could beat the person who opened the door—they wanted you to be first so they could invite you in.

Then they had to offer you the "Christmas give." For the visiting grown-ups this meant thick slices of cake and sassafras tea or wild persimmon beer; for the children it was usually a little handful from a basket of fruits and nuts and candy kept near the door throughout the Christmas season. This little farm-country tradition always made Christmas more fun.

from "Papa's Angels"

COLIN WILCOX PAXTON
and GARY CARDEN

COLIN WILCOX PAXTON
(1935-   )

Colin Wilcox Paxton was born and raised in Highlands, North
Carolina. Drawn to the theatre, she went to New York to pursue
acting and appeared in her first Broadway play in 1958, winning
the Clarence Derwent Award for Best Supporting Actress. She
has appeared on stage in New York, London, and Los Angeles,
and has been in eighty television programs and over fifteen films.
Paxton is best known for her portrayal of "Mayella Violet Ewell"
in the classic movie *To Kill A Mockingbird* (1963). Her other film
appearances include *Midnight in the Garden of Good and Evil*
(1997). Her play, *Papa's Angels*, had several successful stage pro-
ductions, and author Terry Kay suggested to Paxton that she write
a book based on the play. In the following excerpt from the book,
Papa's Angels: A Christmas Story (1996), Becca, a twelve-year old
mute girl, recounts the story of a very special Appalachian
Christmas.

Gary Carden was born and raised in Sylva, North Carolina. He says
he began writing, in part, "to find out how I felt about being
Appalachian." Carden has written several plays based on either
Cherokee myths or local folklore, including *Land's End*. He has
also coauthored *From the Brothers Grimm*, and contributed a
chapter on the mythology of the Southeastern Tribes for *Native
American Myth and Legend*.

*T*his is what happened today and tonight. It is Christmas Eve today and this morning we decided that everything would work out. Maude and John Neal found Momma's Christmas tree decorations. They was back up and under the eaves of the attic in a hidey-hole Momma had up there. They brought them down stairs and laid them all out on the table. Some of them Momma had baked from bread dough and painted, and some of them Papa had whittled. A few were store-bought, like the Angel that goes on top of the tree. And John Neal thought the Angel looked like Momma, 'cause she had long goldie hair jest like the Angel. Alvin said that Momma didn't have no wings growing out of her back. John Neal said, he reckoned Momma had wings now, he bet, and on and on the argument went. Then Alvin said that the Angel was supposed to be the one that come to announce the birth of Jesus. That's when the trouble started.

"Who was Jesus' Momma and Papa?" said Maude. She was asking Hannah Rose since, being the oldest, 'cept me, she was supposed to know.

"Well, Mary was the Momma and this man named Joseph was the Papa," said Alvin.

"No, the Holy Ghost was the Papa," said Hannah Rose. "Joseph didn't even know that Jesus was coming until the Angel told him." "Anyway, forgit about that part. The important part is when they went to pay the taxes and they ended up in this town and couldn't find a place to stay, so they had to stay in a barn."

"And that's where Jesus was born," said Hannah Rose.

"In a barn," said Alvin.

"Like our barn?" said John Neal.

"I guess so," said Alvin.

"And the wise men come," said Hannah Rose.

"And the shepherds who was out watching their sheep," said Alvin.

"How did they know to come and see Jesus?" said John Neal.
"Because of a star," said Hannah Rose. "They followed a star."
"And they was Angels," said Alvin. "Don't forgit the Angels."

"Was there cows and sheep and animals and all like that in the barn?" said Maude.

"Oh, yes," said Alvin. "They got down on their knees and adored Jesus."

"The cows and the sheep did?" said John Neal.

"Yes," said Alvin.

"And the trees too," said Hannah Rose.

"Trees?" said John Neal.

"Yes, the trees come and got down on their knees and worshipped and adored Jesus," said Hannah Rose.

"How does a tree do that?" said Maude.

"Do what?" said Hannah Rose.

"Git down on its knees. Do trees have knees?"

"Oh yes," said Hannah Rose. "They got knees and limbs."

"What kind of trees?" said John Neal. "Oh, pines and cedars and spruce."

"That must have been a real big barn," said Maude. "I mean, if the cows and the horses and the sheep . . . "

"And the Angels," said John Neal. "Don't forgit the Angels!"

"And the wise men and the shepherds and all . . . "

"Did the Angels fly around or did they roost like our chickens do?" said John Neal.

"Angels don't roost, John Neal," said Maude, "They jest keep a' flyin' and a' flapin' around."

"They was flying around singing 'Hallalu-ya!'" said Hannah Rose.

"What was the Baby Jesus doin' while everbody was crowdin' in there?" said Maude.

"Oh, he was jest lyin' in his manger, wavin' his little arms around. He jest loved it," said Hannah Rose.

Then Papa come home. There was the Christmas tree decorations all laid out on the table and he seen them right away. Alvin tried to explain.

"Papa, we know there won't be a Christmas, but we thought there might be a tree," he said.

"Since the tree is allus brought by Santa Claus, and since he don't know we can't have Christmas this year . . . " said Hannah Rose—

" . . . he will bring the tree anyway," said Alvin.

"And so we thought it would be alright to go ahead and pull out the decorations."

Papa just stared at us.

"And since Santa Claus don't know no better . . . " said Alvin—

" . . . he will probably bring the tree," said Hannah Rose—

" . . . not knowing that we ain't having Christmas this year," said Alvin.

Papa stared at us some more. "So you think Santa Claus is coming," he said. We all nodded.

"Since he don't know what you decided," said Hannah Rose.

Papa went to the closet and got the shotgun. He loaded both barrels.

"It's gitting pretty dark out there now," said Papa. "I guess Santa is flying around this holler by now." Then, he walked out the door. We heard both barrels go off behind the house.

Papa come back in and opened the shotgun. Two smoking hulls popped out in his hand.

"I don't know if I hit him or not," said Papa, "but I'll bet I scared him pretty bad. He won't be stopping here tonight! Now, git to bed."

And we went. That's where I am now, writing in my book. Maude cried herself to sleep worrying about Santa Claus, and this seems like the darkest, longest night of the year. When I looked out the window at Chilly Knob, Grammy's light was out.

Now it's a few hours later. Jest after I wrote that Grammy's light was out, I heard a little shuffling noise on the attic steps. Maude was deep asleep, just wore out from crying. So I got up real quiet out of the bed. From the top of the attic steps I could see John Neal tip-toeing down the last step. Then he begun tiptoeing around, putting each little foot down careful as he went, to where Papa was asleep in his chair in front of the fire. Papa's boots was setting by his chair and his legs was stretched out. John Neal creeped up to Papa and by the light from the fireplace, I seen that he had Fuzzy in his arms. He stopped jest afore he got to Papa's chair and begun to pat Fuzzy and whisper to him. He whispered so soft I could barely hear him. He said, "Fuzzy, you and me been friends a long, long time. Long as I can 'member. You're the bestest friend I have in the whole world. But Papa needs you now. You got to go an' be Papa's friend 'cause Papa is real sad. Be his friend. An' make him happy like you make me happy. And then Momma, an' Sandy Claws and all the Angels will come and everthing will be fine like it usta. Now, you don't cry, jest go on and make Papa happy." Then, John Neal held up Fuzzy and kissed him on his nose. "Bye Fuzzy," he said.

Then he done this. He put Fuzzy down and very, very gentle-like he begins to pull off one of Papa's socks. Papa moved in his sleep and John Neal quick as anything scooted around and hid behind Papa's chair. Papa begun to snore again. John Neal come out from behind the chair and begun to pull at that sock till he had it peeled off Papa's foot. He picked up Fuzzy and commenced to stuff him into the sock 'till jest his head was pecking out the top. He give Fuzzy in the sock one last big hug, and laid him down in Papa's lap. An' without looking back, John Neal tip-toed back up the stairs. I got out of sight 'afore John Neal could see me and waited til he got to sleep. Then I went and waked up the others and told them with my signing what John Neal had done. So, they all got their presents for Papa out from where they was hiding them and tip-toed down the stairs and put them in Papa's lap. Hannah Rose had made a match-holder so Papa would allus have matches for his pipe. And there was a new set of guitar strings from Alvin. I jest knew he'd spent every last penny he'd been saving to buy hisself a juice harp like Papa's. Maude had took an apple and stuck it full of cloves and tied it around with a little ole piece of ribbon. She'd watched Momma make 'em lots of times to hang in our clothes closet to make it smell good in there. I couldn't imagine how long it must of taken her, with her little hands, to stick that apple 'round with cloves.

After they all crept back up to bed I knew it was time for me to finish my book, so I set down at the kitchen table, and now I am writing this. We love you, Papa. I'm going to stop now, and leave my present with the rest.

from "The Christmas Letters"

LEE SMITH
(1944–   )

Lee Smith was born in Grundy, Virginia, a small mining town where her father ran the dime store. Reading and writing were an important part of her childhood, and at the age of eight she wrote her first book on her mother's stationery. She attended Hollins College where she studied creative writing with Louis Rubin. Her first novel, *The Last Day the Dogbushes Bloomed* (1968), was written while she was a student at Hollins. Smith says: "I write the last sentence of a book first. I guess that sounds crazy, but that's the way I've always done it. It gives me the long view, I suppose." Smith married poet James Seay and moved to Tuscaloosa, Alabama, where she was a reporter for the *Tuscaloosa News* and wrote two novels, *Something in the Wind* (1971) and *Fancy Strut* (1973). The couple moved to Chapel Hill in 1974, and Smith juggled teaching and writing. *Black Mountain Breakdown* (1980) signaled Smith's return, through her writing, to Appalachia and to more serious subject matter. Smith has received critical acclaim for both her short stories and her novels, including *Saving Grace* (1995). In 1996, Smith published *The Christmas Letters: A Novella* with Algonquin Books of Chapel Hill which was founded by her former teacher, Louis Rubin. Like Christmas tree lights, the family Christmas letter is an American invention. Smith uses this infamous genre to create an epistolary novella journeying into the hearts and minds of three generations of women. In this excerpt from *The Christmas Letters*, Mary Copeland writes from the Greenacres trailer park announcing the birth of a son.

Dec. 26, 1967

*Q*ear Family,

My apologies for mimeographing this letter to stick in your card, but please consider it a very personal Merry Christmas anyway, from me and Sandy and ANDREW BIRD COPELAND who is six months old at this time, almost completely bald but the cutest baby in the whole world according to his proud parents MR. AND MRS. SANDY COPELAND of #20 Greenacres Park, Raleigh, N.C., where we have now moved as Sandy says there is more opportunity here in the building trades.

Greenacres Park is actually a *trailer park*, and we are living in a rented trailer which would not have been my first choice, as it is aqua, but it *is* very reasonable since *everything* is furnished—wall-to-wall carpet (yuck—more aqua!), blinds and drapes at the windows, a built-in bar and stools in the little kitchen, etc. All this is lucky for us since we have started our housekeeping on a shoe-string, you might say. Of course, the size of this trailer *is* a little bit small for Sandy (who is 6'3", after all!). He has to walk around hunched over all the time. But he works so much that he is not home a lot, so it is okay, and will suit us fine until we can afford to move to another place. Actually this trailer reminds me of a doll-house—remember when I "took care of dolls" for Daddy? I was so proud of myself. The big difference is, this little doll house is *real*!

I wonder if everybody is so crazy about their first baby, and so worried about him. Even though Andy is sleeping through the night now, I still wake up every three hours and can't go back to sleep until I have tiptoed over to his crib just to see if he is still breathing, and I'm happy to report that so far, he *is*! And one *nice* thing about the size of the trailer is that I can check on Andy constantly. We are never far apart in here!

When Sandy comes home from work in the evenings, he always asks me what I've been doing all day, and honestly I don't know how to answer this question. "I can't exactly remember," I tell him, "but whatever it was, it just wore me out!"

The truth is with a baby, the time flies. Of course I can remember how, as a teenager in the not-so-distant past, I used to get bored. Sundays, for instance, just dragged on and on. . . . I truly did have "time on my hands" and never even knew it until now, when I don't have any! Who *was* that girl who used to "moon around" (Mama's word for it!) and read so much? I feel like she was somebody else, not me, not this new me who always has something to do. Fold the diapers, feed the baby, burp the baby, put him down, peel the potatoes, pick the baby up and change him, put him in the playpen, put the water on to boil, wash off his pacifier which he has thrown down in the floor, put the potatoes in the boiling water, cut up the chicken, find the pacifier again, wash it off, etc. I won't go on and on, but you can get the general idea!

It is a major expedition whenever we go out, such as to the grocery store or to the laundromat or to the library or the little playground behind the Episcopal Church up the street (St. Michael's). Or we might go visit Susan Blankenship in #11, who has just had a baby girl named Melanie, or Marybeth Green in #45, whose John is actually three months older than Andrew, though of course Andrew is much more advanced and smarter. Andrew really enjoys visiting John. They are so cute—they love to play side by side, though they are not old enough to play together yet. This is called "parallel play"—I keep checking out all those books on child development. Sandy teases me about it, but I am just so *terrified* that I will make a mistake. Some mistakes are irrevocable, a thing I never really realized until I had a baby of my own. This thought scares me to death. I feel like everything I have ever done before means nothing, in comparison to taking care of this baby.

Sandy comes from a family of seven, so he thinks I worry too much. For instance Sandy believes in letting a baby cry, that this develops his lungs, but I can't stand it, snatching Andrew up the very minute he opens his mouth. And let me tell you, his lungs are developing just fine anyway, thank you very much! Sandy tells me all the time that I am spoiling "that baby" but actually he is just crazy about him too, and calls him "Duke." (I'm not sure where he got that name!) "Hey, Duke," Sandy will say, and kind of box with him. They both get the biggest kick out of this little game.

So I want everybody out there to know that I am fine, happy as can be in this little aqua blue shoebox of a home with my baby Andrew. We are so busy in here that it is very difficult right now for me to even imagine any other world outside these four walls.

I watch Vietnam on television, of course, and often think of you, Joe, but honestly it is hard for me to concentrate too long or to believe that the war is actually *real* and not just another show on television. I know that's awful, but it's true. Somehow I believe it would seem more real to me if it *wasn't* on television all the time. Honestly, my imagination has failed me on this. I'm so glad you will be home soon.

But Joe, I *do* wish that you would write, at least to me. I'm sure you are hearing this from all of us, so *do* it! Make copies and send one to everybody, like I'm doing here. I'm sure the army has got a mimeograph machine *someplace*! By the way, it is hard for me to believe you scarcely know Sandy yet. Somehow I think that all the people I love, love each other as much as I love them, and I forget that you all have hardly met.

Well, I will quit running on and on and tell you now about Sandy's and my first Christmas dinner together (yesterday). It was a riot! We had a baked hen which barely fit in my oven (I am *trying*, Mama!) and oyster casserole which did not work out because I used *smoked* oysters instead of the real other kind which I guess you are supposed to use. (I had bought these flat square little cans of oysters at the Piggly Wiggly, they were very expensive and blew my whole food budget for the week, but I thought you *had* to have oyster casserole on Christmas, Mama. I thought it was the law!)

Well, it *looked* okay, the cracker crumbs having formed a nice golden crust just the way they are supposed to, but the minute I bit into it, I knew something was the matter. But Sandy did not even know the difference because he had never tasted oysters before anyway. Luckily, Sandy will eat *anything*, and he thought it was delicious! We ate Christmas dinner on the floor—on our aqua shag carpet, that is!—since we don't have a table yet (though Sandy is going to build us one soon, he can build *anything*, if he can get off from work long enough to do it) while Andrew slept on his blanket right beside us. And when we got up to do the dishes, we saw it had started to snow! So we bundled poor little sleepy Andrew up in that red snowsuit you sent, Mama, and took him out in his first snowfall ever, which was coming down so thick and fast that we couldn't see beyond our little row of trailers, to the street.

The streetlight made a perfect cone of light, full of whirling flakes, as we stood beneath it and stuck our tongues out to catch the flakes and tried to make Andrew stick his tongue out, too. How sweet and cold those snowflakes were, melting on our tongues, I will never forget it.

And then before we knew it, everybody from the other trailers had come out too, and we met neighbors we have never even *seen* before! Such as a crazy old lady named Miss Pike, who wears the most makeup you have ever seen and used to teach singing lessons, opera I believe, and a fat little man named Leonard Dodd who described himself as an "inventor" (thought I don't know what he invents), and another man named Gerald Ruffin who looked very aristocratic, but wore a plaid robe and red velvet bedroom shoes and was drunk as a lord. Somebody whispered that he used to be a lawyer but had fallen on hard times. He was in politics, too. He is from one of the most prominent families in the state. I guess he must be the black sheep of *that* family! We all talked about the snow, and passed around some of the fudge that you sent, Mama, and then the Teeter sisters had us in for coffee. You have never seen as much junk as they have squeezed into their trailer—they call it "brick-a-brack." It covers every surface that is not already covered by a doily. All their coffee cups were made of flowery bone china, with gold rims. Gerald Ruffin's hands were shaking so much that his cup rattled on his saucer like a castanet. Well, I could go on and on. . . . (No doubt this is the same impulse which used to lead me to write *The Small Review!*). Anyway, I don't know whether it was that coffee or pure excitement, but I couldn't sleep a wink all night long. I lay snuggled up to Sandy like a spoon in a drawer and listened to Andrew make his snuffly little sounds in sleep, and peeped out the porthole window at my portion of the sky, which was full of whirling snowflakes, no two alike in the universe, and thought about my baby, and my husband, and Daddy, and all of you, and my heart was full to bursting.

Merry Christmas and love from your very poor but very happy,

Mary Copeland

P.S. I will *spare* you my recipe for my oyster casserole! Oh, I also made a big batch of Sticks and Stones for Sandy to give his boss. They were a big hit. So if Sandy gets that raise he's hoping for, it will all thanks to me, his *wife*, MARY COPELAND!

from "All Over but the Shoutin'"

RICK BRAGG
(1959–   )

Rick Bragg was born in northeastern Alabama, like his mother and
father before him. He says he grew up "in a house in which there
were only two books, the King James Bible and the spring-seed
catalog." Bragg liked to read and remembers the last gift from his
father, a box of books he bought for his son at a flea market. He
says, "I still have those books. I would not trade them for a gold
monkey." Bragg attended Jacksonville State University from
1978–1980 and Harvard University as a Nieman fellow from
1992–1993. He began his journalism career in 1980 at *The
Anniston* (Alabama) *Star* and worked for various newspapers,
including *The Los Angeles Times*, before joining *The New York
Times* in 1994 as a metropolitan reporter. Later that year, he
became a domestic correspondent for *The New York Time's*
Atlanta office. Bragg won a 1996 Pulitzer Prize in journalism,
awarded for his feature writing, "elegantly written stories about
contemporary America." Bragg used the extraordinary gifts for
insight and storytelling that earned him a Pulitzer Prize in writing *All Over but the Shoutin'*, the haunting story of his family's
life and his mother's perseverance. Bragg says, "I wanted to write
a book about my mama. And I think everyone likes a book about
a man thanking his mama." In this excerpt from *All Over but the
Shoutin'*(1997), Bragg recalls bittersweet memories of the
Christmas when he was twelve years old.

I turned twelve in the summer of 1971. I was what I had always
been, the son of a woman who did all she could do on her
own, and needed a little help. I had given very little thought
to being poor, because it was the only realm of existence I knew.
The lives I read about in books or saw on the black-and-white TV

were disconnected somehow, not real. We were never invited into the nicer houses, never shopped in nicer stores. The ritziest place I had ever been inside was the dime store on the old courthouse square. It was run by two ancient sisters. I would walk the aisles, looking at the toys and worthless knickknacks and magazine rack, which I was not allowed to touch. The old women tracked me with their eyes, every step I made. At ten-minute intervals one of the old women would ask if they could help me. "No ma'am," I would say, "I'm just lookin'."

Once, at Christmas, I was looking for a present for my momma. They had some ceramic angels to hang on the wall, spray-painted gold. They broke easy, I guess. I picked one up and turned to the counter and one of the old women met me, saying, "You ain't got enough money for that." To this day I don't know how that old woman knew how much money I had.

I got a lesson in who I was at Christmas, I believe in 1971. A fraternity at Jacksonville State University threw a party for the children of poor families. They bought me a coat, a pair of shoes, a football, and a transistor radio. They held the party in their fraternity house, all the sugar cookies you could handle, and the 7 Up flowed like water. Mark and I sat together, surrounded by strangers, and I drank it all in. I was twelve, but I remember everything about that night. I wasn't old enough to be ashamed about being the charity these glowing young people had gathered around, like a Christmas tree. But I was beginning to realize the difference between me and them.

The men, who called themselves Brothers, drove up with their dates in fastback Mustangs, Camaro convertibles and cream-colored Cougars, high school graduation presents, for sure. The women were all pretty—I cannot remember a time when every single woman in sight had been so damned pretty—and they all smelled very, very nice. They wore sweaters over their shoulders and they kept wantin' to reach out and mess up my crookedy haircut. The men all had on penny loafers and blue jackets with ties, more ties than I had ever seen, and smelled strongly of High Karate. It was like they had a big bottle somewheres and passed it around.

I did not understand the concept of "fraternity," but I knew that these were the rich folks. They were not rich folk by Manhattan standards, merely by Possum Trot ones. They were nice rich folk — they had to be to empty their pockets for children they didn't know — but were as alien to people like me as Eskimos and flying saucers.

These were the sons and daughters of small towns around Alabama and Georgia, the offspring of real estate brokers, insurance barons and English professors. They were members of their town's First Baptist Church, give or take a Methodist or two, and just because they had a six-pack after the JSU Fighting Gamecocks whipped Troy State's ass in football didn't mean they did not love the Lord.

Their Christmas tree was the biggest one I had ever seen, even bigger than the one in church. It was piled three feet high with presents, and after singing "Silent Night" and sipping punch they handed them out to the sons and daughters of pulpwooders and janitors and drunks, who all sat perfectly still, like my brother Mark and me, afraid to move. The jacket they gave me was gray plaid wool, and the transistor radio already had batteries in it.

They were Southerners like me, yet completely different. I remember thinking that it would be very, very nice to be their kind instead. And I remember thinking that, no, that will never happen.

We were part of it, of that night, because we were poor and because we were children, and I like to think that the frat boys and their Little Sisters still do that for the poor children in and around town. But you simply outgrow your invitation into that better world, as your childhood races away from you. You reach the age, ultimately, when that barrier slams down hard again between you and them, and the rest of the nice, solid, decent middle class. Perhaps it wouldn't be so bad, if it was a wall of iron instead of glass.

You see them every day on their side. On their side, the teacher calls their name in homeroom and they walk with their heads up to her desk, to leave their lunch money, and pay their own way. On your side, the teacher calls your name and you stare at the tops of your shoes, waiting for her to check the box beside your name that says "Free," wishing she would hurry. On their side, the summer glows with bronze beauties in bathing suits at the beach. On your side, people step away from you as you wait in line at the hamburger stand, because you smell like sweat and fertilizer and diesel fuel.

On the other side are cars that don't tinkle with the sound of rolling beer bottles, and houses that don't have a bed in the living room. But what really kills you on that other side are the people — the smiling, carefree people — who can just as easily look over into your side, and turn their face away.

Only the oxygen is richer on your side. It has to be. Because your childhood burns away much, much faster.

Acknowledgments

Special thanks to the following individuals for their assistance in making *Southern Christmas* possible:

Richard Abate, Cheryl Andrews, Faith Freeman Barbato, Nancy Bereano, Matthew Bruccoli, Carol Christainsen, Marjorie Conte, Fred Courtright, Matthew Crenshaw, Jeffrey Czekaj, Barbara Thompson Davis, Sean Ferrell, Michael Greaves, Jay Gress, Mindy Koyanis, Kathy Landwehr, Amy Medders, Beth Nevers, Kathy Pories, Theron Raines, Paul Quick, Craig Tenney, Martina Voight, Lee Walburn, and many others, as well as all the wonderful authors.